THE KING'S DAUGHTERS

THE KING'S DAUGHTERS

PJ. CRAM

Copyright © 2024 PJ. Cram

The moral right of the author has been asserted.

Apart from any fair dealing for the purposes of research or private study, or criticism or review, as permitted under the Copyright, Designs and Patents Act 1988, this publication may only be reproduced, stored or transmitted, in any form or by any means, with the prior permission in writing of the publishers, or in the case of reprographic reproduction in accordance with the terms of licences issued by the Copyright Licensing Agency. Enquiries concerning reproduction outside those terms should be sent to the publishers.

This is a work of fiction. Names, characters, businesses, places, events and incidents are either the products of the author's imagination or used in a fictitious manner. Any resemblance to actual persons, living or dead, or actual events is purely coincidental.

Troubador Publishing Ltd
Unit E2 Airfield Business Park,
Harrison Road, Market Harborough,
Leicestershire LE16 7UL
Tel: 0116 279 2299
Email: books@troubador.co.uk
Web: www.troubador.co.uk

ISBN 978 1 80514 332 1

British Library Cataloguing in Publication Data.
A catalogue record for this book is available from the British Library.

Printed and bound in Great Britain by 4edge Limited
Typeset in 11pt Minion Pro by Troubador Publishing Ltd, Leicester, UK

*Thank you to my son Alexander
for his support and encouragements*

Prologue

In 1663, the French King Louis XIV decided to reorganise his colonial empire and set up a royal government in Quebec. La Nouvelle-France had about three thousand French settlers, mainly men. Then, Louis XIV asked Jean Talon, his royal representative in Quebec, to stimulate Quebec's economy by sending more women to settle there and marry.

During this era, most of the men in Quebec made a living by fishing, hunting, fur trading, valeting, joinery and building work. Most of them were hoping to make a fortune before returning to France.

Louis XIV thought that bringing young women over to marry would stop the men from returning to France and encourage them to have a family and settle in Quebec.

Most of the young women sent to Quebec were taken from charitable institutions. They were mainly orphans; however, a few young women had mental illnesses or worked in prostitution.

The king gave each woman sent to Quebec a dowry to facilitate marriage. The dowry was quite generous. It consisted of clothing, needles and thread, a comb, scissors, two knives, a thousand pins, four shoelaces, a bonnet and fifty pounds. It was quite a good dowry for a poor girl and essential for a good marriage.

1

Departure

It was a cold September in 1663 when Marguerite Lafontaine and her younger sister Marie, both orphans, left La Rochelle. Marguerite, eighteen and Marie, fourteen, were very anxious about starting a new life in "La Nouvelle-France". After all, they had heard rumours that Quebec was populated with savages, and the winter lasted over eight months. Their only hope and saviour is to find a husband as requested by the king.

When they both board the boat *Saint-Louis*, it is filled with fear and excitement. The sisters are feeling nervous.

"Will we survive the journey?" says Marguerite

"One month is such a long time." Marie sighs.

They joined another group of sixty girls like them, looking for a better life.

Squeezed in the dirty boat dock, the stench is unbearable.

"I think I am going to be sick," cries Marie.

"Get off the boat!" shouts one of the girls.

"Come and sit next to me," says Marguerite protectively.

They suddenly hear the horn of the boat. The boat sets sail, and they are off.

The following morning, after waking up, they are presented with a meagre breakfast consisting of some wheat mixed with water and milk.

Marguerite tried to think about better times, when her mother was still alive. The family was poor, but she had a loving mother, and they could just manage to feed themselves on the small wage her dad brought home from working as a field labourer in Brittany.

Her mother always sang popular children's songs like 'Alouette', teaching them simple games and giving them cuddles when upset. She remembers her mum chasing them around the field, pretending she was a wolf. Marguerite was scared, but it was exciting and so much fun. If the sun was shining, her mother prepared a picnic, and they usually went to the beach. It was a wonderful memory for Marguerite at the beach with her mother, building sand castles, looking for seashells and racing each other laughing. Marguerite always won the race. Her mother probably enjoyed seeing her beaming face after each win. When her mother died suddenly at thirty-three, her father could not work and look after them, so he decided that the best place for them would be the orphanage. Marguerite was nine years old then, and her sister Marie was five.

The boat was now in the open sea, and the swell of the waves was so bad that most of the girls threw up. The lousy weather remained for six days. Many of the girls were quite sick and could hardly eat the little food they were given.

After ten days of travel, the weather finally settled. By then, four girls had died, partly because they had boarded the ship in poor health. One had a terrible cough, and another had otitis, which could sometimes be fatal.

Another problem started facing the girls. Some men on board were getting restless and pestering the girls for sexual favours. Some men were becoming quite aggressive, and it was difficult for the girls to keep them at bay. Marguerite was very vigilant and made sure to keep her sister and herself safe. She luckily befriended an older crew member called Jean Vignon, who was from the same area as them in Brittany. Jean always treated them as his own daughters and looked out for them.

Eight years in an orphanage had been difficult for Marguerite. Her father visited regularly during the first three years, but they never saw him again. She heard he had remarried and wondered if he had more children. She had never been very fond of her father. In fact, she felt relieved when he stopped visiting. It was always her mother she had missed so much.

Marguerite

Despite the hardship endured on the ship, Marguerite was full of hope. She thought Quebec would be the start of a good life, at least a better life for her and her sister and especially a life with more freedom.

Her time at the orphanage had been burdensome, with the nuns being so strict and devoid of affection. Still, she and Marie had been taught to read and write, a privilege in those days. They also were good seamstresses, which was an excellent skill for young women. Above all, Marguerite was a romantic and hoped to meet a friendly and loving husband, someone very different from her father and the men she had met on the boat. She thought she would make a good wife and, hopefully, be blessed with a large family. She wanted to serve her king, who wished for La Nouvelle -France's population to grow and prosper.

Marguerite knew she was attractive, as many other girls had been jealous of her good looks. She was tall with a generous figure. Her beautiful chestnut eyes matched the colour of her long, curly hair. She had high cheekbones, and when she smiled, you could not resist but smile back. Her skin was flawless and a light, clear honey colour.

Would she meet a fisherman, a fur trapper or a builder? All the men over there were in these trades. She wanted a good man, hard-working but also attentive, taking her in his arms and kissing her when he came home after work.

She thought of her father coming home drunk, always full of anger, swearing and sometimes hitting her mother. Marguerite and Marie would hide under the table or the bed to escape his wrath. Her mother would give them a secret hand signal to hide to protect them from the savagery of her drunk husband. Some mornings, she would find her mother with a black eye or, at worst, hardly able to walk. Marguerite would start crying, and her mother would comfort her, saying, "Don't worry, I am fine."

Her father was the devil himself in more ways than one Marguerite thought. Her father was bringing food to the table, and there was no escape for women with children if they did not want to starve. Men ruled, and a married woman couldn't leave a marriage. It was unthinkable for their mother to do so despite her husband's drinking and violence.

MARIE

At fourteen, Marie was not a dreamer. She had always been very different from her sister, not remembering much about her childhood with her parents, as she was too young when her mother died. Marie recalls, however, how much her sister had protected her and loved her like a mother would. She followed her sister, trusting her completely and agreed to go to Quebec with her.

Compared to her sister, Marie was slightly built with a dainty figure and a lovely pale complexion. Her hair was jet-black, long and straight. She mostly plaited her long hair and formed a chignon at the back of her head. Her piercing sky-blue eyes made her very attractive, and when she smiled, you instantly felt the warmth coming from her.

Marie was a fiery young girl who was expecting much more than marriage. After all, she was the brightest and the best reader at the orphanage. The nuns had coached her privately to teach her history and Latin. She was very proud of it and could not understand why most women wanted to marry or spend their lives dedicated to God. She believed, in fact, that of the two, God was a better bet.

It was the nuns' expectation that one day Marie would become a nun and dedicate her life to God. Marie had other ideas but kept them to herself.

Marie had big dreams about settling in Quebec. She hoped there would be a chance for a girl like her to become somebody and, at fourteen, could further her education and become a teacher or work as a clerk or a nurse. She was unsure what was available for her in this new country, but surely, it could not be any worse than her old world.

She had heard that life in the new world was more accessible and less conventional. Indeed, there would be opportunities for an ambitious and bright young girl like her. Only one thing really troubled Marie: would she be separated from her sister? She loved Marguerite so much, and she was her only family. If Marguerite married as soon as she hoped, would she be able to live close by and see her often?

Marie shed a tear thinking about it. Despite all this bravado, she was worried. She was only fourteen after all, what would happen to her. Starting a new life in such a faraway country was daunting for a young girl.

Almost docking

"We have three more days at sea before arriving in La Nouvelle-France," shouted the captain. By now, fifteen other girls had died during the voyage. Many girls died of scurvy due to lack of vitamin C during long sea crossings. Most of the corpses were thrown into the sea after a very short Catholic ceremony consisting of a few funeral prayers told by a young priest doing the crossing on the boat. Each time, the spirit of the girls was very downbeat, wondering who would survive the trip or which one would die next.

The sea had become wild again. Giant waves were furiously rocking the ship up and down. Thumping and deafening noises were everywhere, coming from the sea and from the passengers.

The rain poured relentlessly all night. The girls could hear it hammering the deck.

Despite the hostile conditions, the boat slowly carved its way through the Atlantic Ocean.

Marguerite and Marie held each other, rolling from side to side in vomit and excrement, unable to stand. Marguerite thought, *we could die*, but kept this to herself, reassuring her sister. The sea was so rough that they could not drink or eat for three days. Both sisters had lost a significant amount of weight.

With her dishevelled hair, her cheeks drawn, and big dark circles under her eyes, Marguerite cried silently, thinking, *no one would want to marry me*. She was a beautiful-looking girl, but she had no confidence and wondered if she would be worthy of finding a husband who would treat her well.

They suddenly heard some shouting on the deck: land! Land! Land!

They had arrived.

The young men who are already in La Nouvelle-France

While the plague raged in many parts of Europe, some young French men decided to try their luck and enrich themselves by crossing the Atlantic. Many of them befriended the local tribes and started to trade with them. Once they were more familiar with this new country, they began selling goods such as knives, pots, sewing needles, tobacco and brandy for beaver pelts but also for mink, wolverine, otter, ermine and fox. Beaver fur was in particular demand throughout Europe. Good quality beaver pelts were, therefore, precious.

Pierre Aubin, Antoine Lemarin and Louis Perrault were three young men who went to La Nouvelle-France to enrich themselves. They were good friends from the same area in Normandy, a small village called St. Aubin. They had done quite well so far, hunting, tracking and fishing. It was their third year in Quebec, and they enjoyed the freedom and their adventures around this vast country.

Pierre was twenty-one when he arrived in Quebec three years previously. He was a tall, robust young man with thick, curly blond hair and was a successful hunter and trapper. Also, he traded sundry and metal manufactured goods with some of the local tribes. With his companions Louis Perrault and Antoine Lemarin, they always ventured further afield. Usually, they returned with the largest and glossiest beaver pelts. They were already famous for their success. Their success, however, was tainted by the fact that they were trading without a licence for a while, and the governor of the colony of New France started to seize a good portion of their furs.

At that time, the King of France wanted to promote farming and settlements to grow the population. Too many men at the start either moved further afield or sailed back to France. The three men had recovered from their mistake and were doing well again.

Pierre was a savvy young man who managed to earn and save a substantial sum of money. He had been able to acquire a large plot of land just west of Quebec and was determined to become a successful farmer. Pierre did not know much about farming but was determined to learn. Like most young men settling in La Nouvelle-France, he needed to find a wife. In his hunting days, he did not think much about girls. Life was exciting and dangerous in the wild and needed all his attention. He also enjoyed going to the taverns, drinking brandy and gambling as most men did after hunting and fishing.

Now, Pierre was ready to change his ways and settle. He eagerly awaited at the Quebec harbour to see the new king's daughters arriving. Pierre was unsure what kind of wife he was looking for as he was inexperienced with women. He was a practical man and wanted someone to help him with the farm. He also looked forward to having a large family with strong and healthy boys and girls.

Their other friend, Antoine Lemarin, was also twenty-four. In fact, they had all come together to Quebec in search of a better life. Antoine was a handsome man, tall, with broad shoulders, a wave of dark hair and a twinkle in his eye. He was funny, and the girls back in Normandy, where he came from, adored him. He had more experience with girls than his shy friend Pierre. While Pierre and Antoine wanted to settle in La Nouvelle-France, Louis looked forward to returning to Normandy a few weeks later. He planned to settle down with his fiancée, who awaited his return.

2

Arrival

When disembarking, Marguerite felt her entire body trembling. She clutched the cross, that her mother had left her, in her hands. It was the only thing inherited from her mother; she wore it on a chain without ever taking it off. The cross was precious to her; she believed it was her good-luck charm, her mother watching over her.

She felt weak after such a long journey. Still, she was also excited they had succeeded and finally arrived in Quebec. Standing on the quayside with the other girls, they were met by Madame Dermont, the lady in charge of helping them settle. Marie was holding her sister's hand tight.

What was the future holding up for the sisters? About one hundred men stood on the quayside, eying up the king's daughters. Who was going to be the one for them?

They were so relieved to arrive on solid ground. Despite the sickness and diseases on the boat and so many girls dying, they had reached the New World. Madame

Dermont gave a speech to welcome the girls. After directing them to the Quebec town hall, she explained that some of them, particularly the youngest, would stay at the convent. The others would remain under the protection of widows or families until they found a suitable husband. All of them would get boarding and lodging.

Marie was terribly nervous; she did not want to be separated from Marguerite. As most settler families were involved with farming, they were looking for strong-built, healthy girls who could help with the farm and the children. Many widows also wanted to take girls who could help and work hard.

The nuns were looking out for the younger ones to stay in the convent until they were old enough to marry or join the convent.

"It feels like being at a cattle market," says Marguerite quietly to her sister.

"I want to stay with you. I could not bear to return to a convent," Marie cries. "I came here with you for a new life, a new beginning. God help us," she murmurs.

As if her prayer was answered, Catherine Cartier approaches the two girls. "Are you two sisters?" she asks.

"Yes, Madame," replies Marguerite shyly.

"Well, I'll take the two of you if you agree to help with the farm and the children. What do you say?"

"Yes, please," answered the girls, smiling. "Thank you, Madame."

Catherine was twenty-eight and already a widow. Her husband had died in a hunting accident. She was left with five little boys to look after, aged between eight and two.

She was actually looking forward to having the two sisters with her, not only for help but also for the company.

Life had been lonely since her husband Henri died a year ago, and though she had received two marriage offers, she had declined. She felt she was not ready to remarry just yet. The two widowers, farmhands, were a great help to her. Her husband Henri had left her quite wealthy, and she could have quickly taken in an indigenous girl to help her with the children and the house as it was the norm, but she preferred not to.

Catherine was a strong and clever lady. She had beautiful red hair and green eyes. The lady was also well educated and well groomed, as her French family belonged to the French gentry. Her parents were very disappointed when she decided to marry Henri, who was well below her social rank. The last straw for them was when they decided to move to Quebec. Her family decided to completely disown her. Her father's final word to her was: "If you decide to move to a place full of savages, don't bother to come back!" Catherine felt sorry for her mother and sister, crying in the background. Still, she never regretted moving to La Nouvelle-France. She had a very satisfying and fulfilled life in Quebec. Her beloved Henri had left her financially comfortable with five beautiful boys.

STAYING WITH MADAME CARTIER

Marguerite and Marie were exhausted when they arrived at Madame Cartier's house. It was a well-built wooden house. It was not very big, but with three bedrooms it was bigger than most. Madame Cartier decided to share a bedroom with her two youngest sons so the two sisters could have their own room. After eating a large bowl of soup with fresh homemade bread prepared by Mme Cartier, the two sisters went to bed and fell asleep almost immediately.

The following day, Marguerite looked out the window and marvelled at the beauty of the place. She could see the forest across the meadow. It was an explosion of warm autumn colours: red spruces, white pines, yellow birch, sugar maples and red oaks. She suddenly felt a rush of happiness and joy. She had made the right choice coming to La Nouvelle-France! *It is stunning!* she told herself.

She excitedly crept out of the room, trying not to wake Marie.

Madame Cartier was sitting at the table with her five boys, eating breakfast. "Come and join us," she said to the girls, smiling. "Help yourself."

Soon after, Marie woke up and sat with them.

"Let me introduce you to my boys," Catherine chirps. "Here is my eldest: Philippe, who is eight, then Baptiste, seven, Robert, five; Nicolas, four and Paul, almost three."

The three youngest boys are looking at the girls, giggling while the two eldest mutter hello shyly. "*Bonjour,*" reply Marguerite and Marie in chorus.

The girls were starving and tucked into their bread and jam. Catherine had also made an omelette with mushrooms for them, knowing the girls had been undernourished during their sea crossing.

"Girls, I will show you around the farm today, but I

don't want you to do any work until you are fully rested."
"We are fine," answered the girls.

"We'll see, tomorrow maybe," answers Catherine. "Philippe and Baptiste, look after your brothers while I take the girls around the farm".

The farm

"My farm is called Les Trois Rivieres. My husband and I decided on the name because we have three streams crossing our land. She pointed them out to the girls. One of the streams was flowing down from the hill behind the farm, and the girls looked with amazement; they had never seen so many springs in one place.

Luckily, after her husband's death, Mme Cartier had been left with a well-working farm. She had the two older farm hands, Jacques and Francois, helping her. The two men lived in a small wooden hut beside her farm and were almost part of the family. They were widowers in their late fifties, and as their children had decided to move west, they gladly accepted to stay at Catherine's farm and help out. It was like having a new family as far as they were concerned, and they doted on Catherine's boys.

The farm had an ox helping to plough the land, five pigs, twenty chickens providing eggs and one noisy and bossy cockerel ensuring a regular supply of new chicks. The chicks could be exchanged or sold at the local market, providing extra income. The three big fields surrounding the farm were planted mainly with wheat, barley, and maise. Alongside and south-facing, a plantation of vegetables, principally cucumbers, corn, peas, and pumpkins, had been planted. It also included a mature orchard with apple, quince and pear trees. At the back of the farm, a small larder was used to keep drying fish and cut wood for the fire.

"Spring, summer and autumn are a hectic time to ensure plentiful supplies for the winter months," comments Madame Cartier. Nearby was a small well used by her two oldest boys, whose daily task was bringing fresh water back to the house.

The girls watch and listen carefully, trying to take everything in. It was undoubtedly a new and different world from the old France they came from. All they knew before was the perimeter of the orphanage or the convent. This place's size and space were beyond anything they could have imagined.

The two sisters settled very quickly at the farm. Marguerite was really enjoying working outdoors, helping the men with the plantations and looking after the chickens and pigs. She loved the pigs and decided to give them a name. During feeding time, she called each of them: "Coco, Fifi, Prunella, Billy, Lulu, come here." They would look up and run towards her to feed. Marguerite thought they were so comical. Lulu especially was the most amiable; she would come close and let Marguerite rub her leathery snout.

Marie preferred looking after the boys and helping with the cooking and housework.

Madame Cartier was strict but also kind and fair.

It was only a month since their arrival, but already, the girls felt safe and happy there. Both girls looked healthily radiant, having put some weight on after such an awful sea crossing. Marguerite was delighted to spend time on the farm and got on really well with the two farmhands. The two old men treated her like a daughter.

"You are a natural," they kept telling her, praising her efforts and quick learning.

Marguerite loved being outdoors and working the land. Most evenings, she enjoyed knitting while chatting to Marie and Madame Cartier.

However, Marguerite was also looking forward to the ball next Saturday, organised for all the king's daughters who had made it to Quebec the previous month. She kept telling her sister, "Will I meet my prince charming? I cannot wait."

Marie, on the other hand, was worried. She felt too young for the ball and was in no hurry to marry. Marie did not feel pressured despite the fact many girls her age did. She had been under pressure to go to the ball, particularly from Madame Dermont, whose duty was to find wives for the men. Marie, however, was thrilled to stay at the farm. She planned to stay with Catherine as long as she could. Fortunately, Catherine had convinced Madame Dermont that Marie was needed at the farm for now. Marie's biggest fear, however, was the idea of losing her sister. Quebec was such a big country that Marie wondered if, once married, Marguerite would move far away with her new husband and she would lose touch with her sister. It was a very frightening prospect for her.

The ball

As promised, Madame Dermont had made sure to invite all the young women eligible and the single men to the town-hall ball. She wanted to fulfil her duty and try to get as many young couples to marry and make a life in the New World. The men far outnumbered the women at the ball, which also meant that almost all the young ladies would find a husband. Marguerite was wearing a beautiful dark green gown that Catherine had lent her. The top of the dress was made of lace with a high neck and fitted her perfectly after a few adjustments made by her sister Marie. All the thirty-five girls stood there in a line facing the men. Madame Dermont walked along the line, introducing the name of each of the girls. Some of the young women blushed. Others were giving the men the eye and smiling. Marguerite did neither. She looked around shyly, noticing that quite a few men were staring at her. The band had two violins, two fiddles and one harp player. Dancing was very popular and fashionable. Everyone was eager to dance the latest steps in vogue in Europe.

Antoine did not waste any time, and as soon as he heard the music, he approached Marguerite. "I am Antoine Lemarin. Would you like a dance, Mademoiselle?"

They started dancing and chatting, getting to know each other. They spent all evening together, oblivious to the rest of the world, laughing and teasing one another. Marguerite could not believe her luck. What a handsome man, witty and charming. Was he really interested in her? He talked about hunting and fishing and how he loved his life in Quebec.

He told her how he would love to settle in this great country full of beautiful lakes and forests. He quickly suggested she could be the woman he had been waiting for.

The ball stopped just before midnight, and by then, many couples had formed; each couple planned to see each other again very soon. After all, it was the King's wish to have as many settlers as possible marrying and producing many children to enhance the population of the French colony. Madame Dermont was very satisfied that evening; the ball went very well. Most of the girls found a suitor except for two or three girls who had not. She hoped every couple who met on the night would marry very soon. She could then report back to the king's court, informing them of the progress.

The French church run by the Jesuits also keeps a very accurate register of all marriages, birth and death.

Marguerite went back home so excited. Catherine and Marie were waiting for her to hear all her news. Marguerite could not stop talking about the ball and the man she danced with all evening; she was over the moon.

"I think I met the man of my dreams," she said, beaming.

"That's wonderful," says Catherine. "Be careful, though; you must try to get to know him better before you commit. There are a lot of untrustworthy men around."

"Of course," replied Marguerite.

Marie did not say much; she smiled, as she was happy for her sister and did not want to spoil her happiness, but she was worried about her sister starting a new life without her.

"We are meeting again next Saturday; I cannot wait!" said Marguerite, smiling.

Antoine told Pierre, "I met the most wonderful girl. I am in love." He spoke dreamily. "I think I am ready to settle; she is beautiful, bright and funny," he added.

Pierre nodded with approval but deep down felt very sad as he also thought Marguerite was fantastic. At that very instant, he wished he was Antoine, confident, charming Antoine. Pierre had not found the girl for him, but he had yet to make much effort, as the competition was fierce between the men. Fewer women than men made it difficult for a shy man like Pierre to engage.

For a month, Antoine and Marguerite met every Saturday, and their relationship went from strength to strength. They got to know each other and kissed a few times, starting to make plans for their future together. Eight weeks after their first meeting, Antoine asked Marguerite for her hand in marriage. Antoine, behaving as a gentleman, had first talked to Mme Cartier and Marie to get their approvals. Catherine and Marie were very fond of Antoine and delighted with the forthcoming wedding.

Marie was reassured she could stay with Catherine and see her sister whenever she wanted. Antoine and Marguerite had planned to stay in this area, which was such a relief for Marie.

A date was fixed for the wedding. It was the twenty-fifth of December, Christmas Day. Marguerite was thrilled, though a bit anxious. She was well aware that Antoine would be away for long periods of time hunting and fishing, and she would miss him so much. She brightened up, thinking he would be around most of the winter months, helping her and cosying up around a warm fire. Antoine told her that he was keen to continue to work hunting for furs. He was not ready to work full-time as a farmer; besides, he had yet to buy land like Pierre and thought he would make more money by selling furs and fishing.

Something that really worried Marguerite even more was going through her first wedding night. Marguerite was fearful of what happened in the past; she never told anyone; she was too ashamed that it was not her first time, and she was not a virgin as expected from a young woman partly brought up in a convent. It had to remain her secret.

The wedding: Christmas Day

Marguerite looked beautiful. She wore a dark red dress, again borrowed from Catherine, and a little matching cape her sister had made for her. She also wore a ribbon in her hair and brown leather shoes under her long dress. Around her neck, she wore a little chain with a small cross. Her mother gave it to her, and she never took it off. It comforted her greatly, thinking her mother was watching over her and her sister. Marguerite felt it was her good-luck charm and would stay close to her heart forever. She told herself that one day, she could pass it on to her own daughter.

It was a freezing winter. The snow outside the church was a meter high, and the men had dug a path for the wedding party. It still was a beautiful scene. The trees were covered with snow, and the church taker had lit candles leading to the church. People were singing hymns, and a man in the church played the organ.

Antoine looked very smart, too. He had borrowed a black suit that used to belong to Catherine's husband, and his dark hair combed backwards emphasised his delicate features. Antoine and Marguerite made their wedding vows, committing themselves to love and respect one another, to be faithful and care for each other. The priest blessed their union with a prayer. The ceremony ended with a beautiful church hymn. When both newlyweds signed the register, Marguerite wrote down her name next to Antoine, who had put a cross as most people then could not read or write.

Antoine was very proud of his wife and thought she was so clever to be able to read and write. It would be such an asset; she could teach their children once they started a family. "The future is bright and promising, my love," he murmured to Marguerite.

They walked out of the church as husband and wife and were congratulated by the entire congregation with good wishes. Marguerite felt she was the heroine of a fairy tale. *It was a magical day*, thought Marie; she was now really happy for both of them. Pierre was pleased to see them so happy but felt slightly sad and jealous of Antoine. He wished he had been the one marrying this beautiful girl, Marguerite; he loved her so deeply as he got to know her better. Pierre made sure nobody else knew about his feelings for Marguerite, and it had to remain so.

With the help of Madame Dermont, Catherine had prepared a small feast in the town hall for the wedding party. It was a joyous event with plenty of food and dancing, and everyone was delighted for the young couple. The party went on well into the night, and even the arrival of fresh snow on the path did not spoil the evening.

Pierre, with the help of Louis and other friends, had built a small wooden house on his land next to his for the young couple. He had told Antoine, but it would be a complete surprise for Marguerite, as she thought they would stay with Catherine for a while as a couple. Catherine had suggested it.

After the wedding, Antoine took Marguerite in his arms and kissed her gently. "I have a surprise for you, Madame Lemarin," he said, smiling broadly. Marguerite could not believe it when Antoine took her to their own house.

She started crying with joy, bewildered. "What a wedding present!" she shouted excitedly.

Pierre and his friends had been so kind.

It was a modest house with just two rooms, but it was their own with a kitchen and a bedroom. It was really a luxury for a young couple just starting. Most couples were not so lucky. Antoine had promised Pierre to give him some of the beaver furs after the next hunting season in return for his kindness and generosity. Marguerite could not believe her luck as they lay down for their first night together in their own house.

Antoine started kissing gently down her neck and then kissing her breasts, caressing them simultaneously. She felt shy and nervous, but her trembling body felt so aroused. Antoine then started caressing her between her thighs. She shivered with pleasure and anticipation; he was very gentle, taking his time and allowing Marguerite to relax. She closed her eyes, so content as she never thought it could be so enjoyable. When he penetrated her gently, it felt so natural that all her fears evaporated. They both climaxed at the same time. "I love you, Madame Lemarin." said Antoine.

"It is the best day of my life. I love you, Antoine," she answered softly. Marguerite was so relieved that Antoine never noticed or asked questions about her past. She doubted what she could have said to him as it was her secret, her shame, and no one should ever find out.

The next day was eventful. They made love a few times again and decided to get their new home sorted. Marguerite went back to Catherine's house to get her belongings. She told Marie about her first night with Antoine and how happy she was.

Mme Cartier also gave her a few things for the house: a sheet and a blanket, a couple of pans, a bag of sugar, a bag of flour and lard.

Marie

Life with Catherine Cartier was going so well for Marie. She started teaching the two older boys to read and write every afternoon for one hour. Philippe, the eldest, was making outstanding progress, always very inquisitive and memorising quickly what Marie was teaching him. She started with the alphabet, and soon, Philippe could write his name and pick out a few words in the bible. Philippe was relatively short and small built for his age, but he was an attractive boy with lovely big brown eyes and dark curly hair. He was a studious and conscientious boy, always wanting to help and please.

On the other hand, Baptiste was finding learning to read really hard. Marie wondered why such a lively young boy, so active and clever when helping with the chores on the farm, was struggling to learn. On many occasions, Baptiste lost his temper, saying that all the letters did not make sense to him. Marie was gentle and patient with him, but it did not appear to make much difference. On the other hand, he loved it when she told him long fairy-tale stories, and he could remember and memorise all the characters. Baptiste had a charming presence, auburn hair and green eyes like his mother. Marie loved his cheeky and fiery personality, and he made her laugh with his pranks and funny remarks.

Marie also liked playing and attending to the younger children; they all loved her and called her "Mimi". Five-year-old Robert was relatively quiet and shy, but the two younger boys, Nicolas and Paul, constantly wanted her attention:

"Mimi, come and play with us."

"Mimi, Paul kicked me."

Marie did not mind; she was so fond of them. Mme Cartier was so grateful to Marie that she could spend more time working on the farm and selling some of her goods at the market. She could stock up for the cold winter months with the extra money. In the evening, once the boys were asleep, they would both do seamstress work: dresses and even hats commended by the more affluent ladies of Quebec and wool clothing that could be sold at the market.

Catherine would talk about her late husband. "I really miss Henri. He was such a good husband," she would say most nights, reminiscing about their good times together. 'Henri made me laugh; he was funny, loving, and so kind to me and the children," she would add sadly. Marie talked about her childhood and life at the convent and how kind and caring Marguerite was to her, more a mother than a sister.

Twice a week, Marie had been asked to go to the Ursuline convent to teach some young children to read. She was so proud to be asked and to be able to help some of the children who were orphaned like her to have a better life. *Education is everything*, she thought. Until now, only children from wealthy noble families, especially boys, were tutored, usually privately. She was hoping one day, it could be all children. She felt very proud she had acquired so much knowledge at the orphanage with the nuns. She was disappointed, however, as she could only teach girls briefly at the convent. The girls, aged between eleven and twelve, were tutored by the nuns and Marie for a short time until they were ready to receive communion.

In most cases, the girls would have needed to be longer in education to learn to read and write. After their communion, the girls had no choice but to learn the basic manual skills: sewing, spinning, knitting and delicate embroidery. They were all destined to get married.

Marie started to believe she could really have a good life in Quebec. She, above all, wanted to make a difference and help all the children who did not have a good start in life. She was also so happy because she could see her sister regularly.

3

Settling in

The Catholic Church, mainly run by the Jesuits in Quebec, had also decided to convert the local indigenous tribes to Christianity. Until now, the relationship between the French settlers and the predominant Huron tribes in this area consisted of trade and alliances against the English.

One day, Marie was asked by the nuns to go and teach French to the son of the Huron's chief. His name was Bidzill, and he was the oldest of the Huron chief's sons; he had just turned eighteen and was destined one day to replace his father as leader. Bidzill looked much like his father, tall and muscular with long dark hair and piercing eyes. He was an excellent horse rider and hunter. His father thought he had all the qualities to replace him in the future and named his son "Bidzill" because it meant strong in the Huron language. Bidzill was wise, thoughtful, caring and strong, perhaps slightly shy. Still, he could also be determined and commanding when it was necessary.

Marie was very apprehensive when she arrived on her first day to teach at the Indian camp. One of the chief aids had come to pick her up, and she had been, for the first time, riding on a horse, sitting a bit frightened behind the rider, holding on tight to him. Marie was introduced to Bidzill.

"*Bonjour, je suis Marie,*" she says.

He stares at her, nods, acknowledging he understood, and answers, "Bidzill," and more slowly, "Bidzill."

Marie smiles and realises she will have much to teach him, as his French is almost non-existent. Marie becomes aware she has never taught French before to someone without knowledge of the language. She feels unprepared and will have to use all her ingenuity for the task.

She starts with straightforward phrases: "*Je m'appelle Marie.*"

He repeats very carefully several times, "*Je m'appelle Bidzill.*"

She continued for over an hour teaching him some basic French.

"*Je suis une femme.*" And Bidzill repeats, "*Je suis une femme.*"

She bursts out laughing. "*Non tu es un homme,*" and she points to herself, "*moi je suis une femme, toi un homme.*"

Eventually, Bidzill manages to say, "*Je suis un homme.*"

It is not easy to master French grammar and understanding, especially when there is no translation. Marie uses a lot of body language to help him understand.

Marie was relieved when the hour of teaching finished; she enjoyed the challenge, but it was hard work for her. "Bidzill is a good pupil, but I'll need to prepare better and find new ways to teach him vocabulary and phrases as I don't speak his language," she told herself.

"*Au revoir, a bientot,*" she says as they part.

"*Au revoir,*" Bidzill manages to repeat with a smile. Marie arrives home content but exhausted, telling Catherine about her exciting day with Bidzill.

Marguerite

Marguerite was very content. She had been married just over three months, and Antoine was an attentive and loving husband. Both of them were helping Pierre at the farm, preparing for planting and sawing, hoping for a good wheat crop in the autumn. Antoine and Pierre went fishing together once a week, enjoying their outings and friendship.

Antoine, however, was also getting ready to go hunting and fishing with Louis up north during the spring and summer months. Marguerite was a bit anxious about losing him for a few months. Still, she knew it was necessary to get supplies of fish, meat and furs to sell and face the following winter. On the other hand, Marguerite also looked forward to spending more time with Catherine and Marie. She had made a few friends in Les Trois Rivieres and acquired a few customers buying the dresses and hats she had made during the winter months. Pierre was also very kind and would be there if she needed help.

The day arrived when Antoine had to leave. Marguerite cried, and Antoine reassured her, kissing her gently. "It won't be long before I am back, my love, don't worry."

She smiled back at him, and he went. It was only a few weeks later she realised she was expecting a baby. She could not wait to tell Marie and her friends but was worried and sad she would have to wait so long for Antoine's return. She was sure he would be delighted as they discussed having a big family. It was now the end of April, and Antoine was due back sometime in September or perhaps earlier, depending on their catch.

After his departure, Marguerite settled into a routine. She helped Pierre with his farm twice a week, planting maise, pumpkins and various vegetables. One of her favourite tasks was feeding the chickens and collecting the eggs. She enjoyed cooking dinner for Pierre and the farmhands who came to work. She thought Pierre was the best friend in the world; he was fun and a good listener when she was worried about Antoine being away, perhaps even thinking he was in danger. He would reassure her, saying, "He'll be alright. I worked with Antoine for three years; the lad is strong and resourceful, and he'll be back soon."

She continued helping Catherine at the farm three times a week. She enjoyed the chatter and was grateful to get fresh bread three times a week. Catherine made fresh bread daily to feed her family; she used a small outdoor stone bread oven. Marguerite also enjoyed the company of Catherine's boys, who were very fond of her and Marie.

Marguerite spent time with them every time she visited, playing and telling them stories.

She liked speaking to Catherine, particularly about her pregnancy.

"What is it like? Is it painful?" she kept asking.

Catherine was very reassuring and kept telling her: "Don't worry, you will be fine. You might be tired and uncomfortable occasionally, but that's normal."

What bothered Marguerite most was whether she would be a good mother? Would Antoine still love her as much after having a baby? Most men, she had heard before, wanted their firstborn to be a boy. Would she be able to deliver?

The rest of the week, she kept busy clothes making and helping Pierre on the farm. She felt she could also confide in him about her pregnancy and fears of being up to the challenge of motherhood. He was most supportive and reassuring, telling her to rest and look after herself.

She was always teasing him, "You are such a good person; you must find yourself a nice girl." Little did she know that Pierre was in love with her. Pierre, however, was pleased about their closeness and friendship. Seeing Marguerite every day was enough for him. Pierre was a very fervent Catholic with strong moral standards. He believed in family values and respected the rules and demands made by the Church.

It was now June, and the weather was beautiful; Marguerite was blooming and highly proud of her prominent bump. She saw Marie most days and could not wait to hear all her stories of teaching at the orphanage, but what she enjoyed most was her sister telling her about Bidzill, who, according to Marie, was making significant progress with his learning. She also loved when Marie was telling her all about the Indians' customs and traditions.

"You know they revere their ancestors, and they have wise people they call shamans. These wise people play a great role in the tribe. They seem to have foresight and advise the chief on everything. They smoke a shared pipe in many celebrations, birth, marriage, and death. They also smoke to get into a trance-like state to help them make decisions." Marie was also describing their village. "They live in wooden huts, which are surprisingly big and high. They are made of stakes and poles covered with elm barks."

She continued enthusiastically, "They are very comfortable and tidy inside with animal skins to sit or sleep on and an area where they store their food and eat, as well as an area to make fire." She was unsure but believed large families lived and shared accommodations, and inside were draping to separate quarters. She was very impressed; not at all what she had expected.

Marguerite was delighted to see her sister settling in and happy. She was now almost seven months pregnant and wondered if Antoine would return on time for the birth. Her heart was longing, and could not wait for his return. She also worried about him. Is he safe? Hunting, tracking and fishing could be dangerous.

Meanwhile, both sisters were helping Catherine with the farm and the boys. Lately, Catherine was worried because Nicolas, her four-year-old, was poorly, and he had a bad cough. Catherine hoped the warmer weather would help, but yesterday, she was alarmed when blood spots stained his little handkerchief. She put him to bed to rest, and the girls took turns to read him stories and keep an eye on him.

Marie taught Philippe three mornings a week, and he was making excellent progress. He could now read and write almost fluently and had a good head for numbers, learning to add and subtract. It was an exceedingly valuable skill to possess if the boy was to become a trader or a shopkeeper; Philippe was so good with mental arithmetic without writing the numbers. He kept asking the girls, "Please give me two big numbers to add," and he was so quick to give an answer. Marie was so proud of him. On the other hand, Baptiste was still struggling with his reading, and Marie had given up teaching him to write. Baptiste, however, had a fantastic memory and was so clever when it came to finding practical solutions for the farm. Catherine had complained a few times when she found broken eggs and missing chickens because they were eaten by foxes. Baptiste decided, with help from the farm hands, to build a coop with perches for them. He did such a good job. They were all proud of him.

Marie

Marie had been teaching Bidzill for over two months now, and he was getting so good with his French that they could have small basic conversations now. She also felt she was learning so much from him about Indian life; she was fascinated. After all, their way of life was not that different from the French settlers. The women attended to the plantations growing maise, pumpkins and fevers. They also made clothes and rugs with animal skins. The men went hunting and fishing and traded tea, tobacco, butter or firearms with the settlers. The Indians also ate similar game like venison and wild birds, but in Quebec, they especially liked eating fish, which was plentiful in the area.

She was getting very fond of the Indian community; they were all friendly and kind towards her, and one of Bidzill's little sisters had made her a bead bracelet. She was delighted to get it.

Marie also loved listening to the old Indian wisdom tales Bidzill was telling her. One she mainly thought was profound says: "We have two wolves inside us. The first wolf represents serenity, love and kindness, and the second represents fear, avidity and hate. 'Which one wins?' asks the child. The one you feed is the answer."

Marie thought it was such a meaningful and wise tale, she would not forget it. It was such a good metaphor for nurturing and being kind. She felt in her heart that Bidzill was definitely the first wolf! She now could not wait each week to meet Bidzill, as they were becoming very close. She never thought it would happen to her, but she was falling in love with him and believed in her heart he felt the same way. *This could not be happening. It would not be allowed, she thought.*

4

The Return of Antoine

It was now September when Antoine returned from his hunting and fishing trip. The hunting had been excellent, and they had plenty of furs to trade and meat for the winter months. The fishing had been plentiful, too; it was a good year for them. Antoine and Louis were full of stories of what happened to them in the wild. Some funny, others more about brutal competitions between hunters. There were also more dramatic stories of meeting Native Indian tribes, particularly the Iroquois and others they were not familiar with. Still, as long as you had something to trade with them, you could negotiate your safety.

Antoine was delighted about the forthcoming birth and thought it was the most beautiful present for his return. Marguerite was so pleased he felt that way. Only two weeks after Antoine's return on the twenty-fourth of September, their beautiful little boy was born. They called him Joseph, which was the name of Antoine's father. The baby was healthy and weighed almost six pounds.

Antoine was so happy and proud of his firstborn, named after his father. "Just rest, love. I am here, and I can help," he kept telling Marguerite. She felt exhausted after the birth and could see everyone fussed around her. She could not quite understand why, but she did not feel that warm, loving feeling towards her baby that so many of her friends had told her about.

She thought, *What's wrong with me?*

All she felt was this big black cloud hanging over her head. She was breastfeeding Joseph every two hours. He was crying a lot, and she was exhausted. Antoine helped a lot, changing the nappies, washing and taking Joseph for little walks in the sun. Marie and Catherine brought food and helped Antoine. Marguerite started crying a lot, thinking she was such a bad mother. *I don't feel anything towards Joseph.* She could not shift all her black thoughts and wished her mother was around to help and make sense of it. For some unknown reason, the dark secret she hid from everyone for so long was playing on her mind. There were voices in her head telling her, "Antoine and Joseph don't deserve you". She did not want to carry on living; life did not make sense to her just now.

At the end of October, it was autumn in Quebec, and the season turned into a beautiful Indian summer. It was sunny and still warm, and the trees were a symphony of autumn colours; the beauty was spectacular. It was six weeks since Joseph's birth, and Marguerite's dark thoughts started to shift. Joseph began to sleep better, and feeding times were less tedious. She started to smile again and talk and sing to Joseph. Everyone was relieved to see her being her own self again and paying much more attention to Joseph. Antoine was a great father and tried to spend as much time as possible with his newborn when he was not working on the farm with Pierre. Marguerite caught him a few times talking to his son: "I'll teach you to fish and hunt, my son. We'll make a great team one day!"

Marguerite could not have expected a better father for her son; her own father had been such a bad example.

They were all settling for the winter months. The harvest and hunting had been so plentiful that Marguerite and Antoine decided to organise a small party for their friends on Christmas Day to celebrate their first wedding anniversary and the arrival of their little boy Joseph. They wanted to thank all their friends for their support.

It was the beginning of December, and everyone was excited about the Christmas party. There were now four feet of snow in Quebec, and the temperature was minus twenty.

Catherine, however, was getting really worried about Nicolas, who had just had his fifth birthday in November. His health and cough had been much better during the warm summer, but he suddenly became very ill and remained bedded for the last three days.

"I am hot, Mummy; why is there blood when I cough?" he asked Catherine a few times and then would doze off again. It was heart-wrenching to see him so poorly, and everyone felt so helpless.

Marguerite and Marie took turns to help Catherine and spend time looking after Nicolas, sponging him to get his temperature down and reassuring him when his coughing spells became more and more frequent and severe. On the fifth day, one of the nuns from the convent came to stay with Catherine, who was exhausted and beside herself. Sister Violette prayed a lot for the child and helped with the chores.

It was on the morning of the ninth of December that, sadly, little Nicolas passed away. It was not uncommon to lose a child. Many parents have lost babies or young children through childbirth or illnesses. However, it did not make it easier for Catherine and her sons. Nicolas's brothers were all heartbroken, and Catherine was so distraught she could not console them. Marguerite, Marie, Antoine, Pierre and the two farm workers all rallied around to support Catherine and the boys. Catherine's world was shattered. She could not even cry, though she was grief-stricken.

Philippe and Baptiste remained quiet for a few days, absorbing the news and very upset to see their mother so lost.

There was a small church service for the funeral, and Father Simon's words during the sermon had comforted them all. It was such a painful time for Catherine; she had difficulty spending time with her sons. She prayed a lot and spent much time going to the church, kneeling and crying. She kept thinking of his sweet little face and big brown eyes and tried remembering their good times together. He was the most gentle and caring son, and when he laughed, it was contagious; everyone would laugh with him.

Marie and Pierre took turns to cheer up the boys, playing with them and talking to them. It was hard for them, particularly the two eldest, Philippe and Baptiste. Pierre was particularly good with them. He was patient and encouraged them to talk about their little brother. Pierre was a good listener, kind and funny, and as a man, was a good role model. He took them outdoors in the cold winter mornings to build snowmen and igloos and slide on the ice. The boys loved it.

Pierre kept telling the boys, "Nicolas can see us and must be laughing with us." These words comforted the boys, and it was not long before Pierre could hear the two youngest mentioning their brother's name while playing.

"Look, Nicolas, I can slide better than Robert."

"Nicolas, look, we built an igloo."

Robert was the one, however, who seemed to miss Nicolas most of all. He was a shy boy who had become more withdrawn and quieter since his brother's death. They had been close and played a lot together. He could not help repeating and asking, "Will I never see Nicolas again? Why?"

It was a challenging and scary thing to comprehend for a young child.

It was now the twentieth of December. Marguerite and Antoine wanted to cancel their Christmas celebrations after such a sad event; however, Catherine would have none of it. She was still very depressed but was slowly realising life still goes on and her boys needed cheering up; they needed her.

Christmas celebrations

The celebrations were a low-key affair after the loss of Nicolas.

A beautiful festive dinner was laid on the table with homemade rye and wheat bread. Poultry was also on the table. It was a real treat, as meat was a luxury. Many vegetable dishes preserved for the winter months were displayed: carrots, lentils, leeks and turnips. As a contribution, Catherine had baked a cake for dessert, to the children's delight. All the adults drank a little wine, and by the end of the dinner, everyone seemed happier and relaxed.

Pierre played a few tunes on his flute, and Catherine's boys started dancing around the table. Little baby Joseph was sound asleep, oblivious to all the noise going around him.

Catherine was smiling, and it was the happiest they had seen her since losing Nicolas. Her boys seemed delighted, too, partly due to seeing their mother cheering up.

The party was a good idea after all. It ended with a toast to Marguerite and Antoine's wedding anniversary and the birth of little Joseph.

Marie was having a good time, too, but just wished Bidzill had been with her here to celebrate. She had not seen him since November because of the snow and was missing him terribly.

She was apprehensive about the future. She knew they had strong feelings for each other, but would they ever be allowed to marry and live together? As far as she understood the Indian community, Bidzill, the chief's son and future leader, was destined to marry an Indian girl from another clan. She also wondered, as a French Catholic girl, if she would ever be allowed to marry a native who had not been converted to Catholicism yet. She thought the whole situation looked doomed for them.

She knew it was possible for Frenchmen settlers to marry Indian women as there was a shortage of women among the French colonists. She had, however, not heard of the reverse happening.

She now could speak Bidzill's Huron language; she had been a quick learner, and she had been asked a couple of times to be an interpreter for trading between the tribes and the local settlers.

If she was rejected by her own French Catholic community, would it be enough to be accepted by the elders and the father of Bidzill?

She also felt pressured by the nuns, sometimes saying to her, "If you are not going to marry, will you become one of us?" The sisters at the convent were lovely to her, and she was so grateful she had been asked to teach. She was lucky to be granted access to the convent's library. She could borrow books, which was an immense privilege for a girl like her of modest origin. Most books were about Christianity, but some were about history, philosophy and medicine. She felt she was always learning something new, and she loved it. She was a very bright young woman, and her thirst for knowledge was insatiable. Reading had been her refuge during the winter months when she missed Bidzill so much.

5

Beginning of a new year

It was now the end of January. Outside, the freezing air was still taking your breath away, and there were still four feet of snow on the ground. Nevertheless, the sun was shining most days, and everyone was looking forward to the beginning of the snow melt, usually starting in March. Snow melting in March created big, messy puddles for a week or two. Still, it was a welcome relief when it was finally over, and everyone was looking forward to the spring and warmer weather.

March was always a mixture of excitement and dread for the population. On one hand, everyone was looking forward to nature's rebirth and warmer weather. On the other hand, everyone hated the melting of the snow, which created for a couple of weeks mud and dirt every time one stepped out of the house. The worst outcome people feared was flooding in their homes, as it sometimes was the case.

A lot of things have been happening in the last few weeks.

First, Antoine had announced that Marguerite was expecting another child due sometime in July. They were both over the moon, though Antoine thought he probably would miss the birth as he would be away during the summer months. Marguerite was a bit anxious about coping with two very young children. She was also concerned about the dark clouds and moods which had affected her after Joseph's arrival. Marie and Catherine reassured her they would be there for her, and Catherine, as an experienced mother, said, "No two births are the same, you know. Each of my boy's birth was different, and usually, it becomes easier," she added.

Marguerite was relieved, and as long as she had the love and support of Antoine, she felt completely safe.

The other big news that surprised everyone was that Catherine and Pierre planned to marry in the spring, probably April, once they had spoken to their priest. Although Catherine was a few years older than Pierre, she was still at a childbearing age. They had grown closer after Nicolas's death. Catherine had been so impressed with Pierre's kindness and support and the care and attention he had given to her boys while she was grieving the loss of her little boy Nicolas.

Everyone was delighted to hear the news and looked forward to the forthcoming wedding. Catherine's boys were overjoyed about it. They were fond of Pierre, and their mother looked much happier.

The only exception was Philippe, her eldest son, who would be eleven in May. Philippe liked Pierre, but as the eldest son, he had enjoyed being the man of the house. He did help a lot on the farm, and being a responsible boy, his mother often asked for his opinion.

"You are my little man; you are so reliable and wise for your age. What would I do without you?" she told him many times. He was very proud of his position as the eldest boy in the family.

The other thing that bothered Philippe was that he still remembered his father, and it was hard for him to see his mother like another man so much. Being close to Marie and trusting her, he had confided in her about his feelings, and she had tried to reassure him. "Pierre is a very kind and thoughtful man who will look after you all. You are in good hands, and it will be good for you, Philippe, not to have so many responsibilities; you are still just a boy," she said to him. She, however, understood how he felt as he had loved his father so much and was devastated when he died.

He listened to Marie and said: "You are probably right. Besides, I like Pierre. He is a kind man and good to us. I just feel a bit jealous that he is spending so much time with Mum."

Marie was returning from the convent on her way back to Catherine's farm. She heard her name being called. She turned around, and to her amazement, she saw Bidzill smiling at her. He had walked all the way from his village to see her. It had taken him half a day wearing his racket snow shoes and riding a sledge to come and see her. She was over the moon to see him and restrained herself from putting her arms around him.

He said, "I'll walk you back." They started chatting like they had never been apart.

She told him all the latest news and how she missed him.

"I missed you so much, my Elu," he replied. "I could not wait another day."

"Elu, what does it mean?" she asked.

"It means 'beautiful' in my tribe," he replied.

"I like it," Marie said, smiling and flattered. "But what are we going to do about being together?" She sighed.

They arrived at the farm, and as Catherine saw them outside, she opened the door and shouted, "Come in, both of you. It is too cold to stay outdoors."

Catherine knew how much Marie cared about Bidzill and was curious to meet him. "I have made some hot tea," she said to them. "Here you are, it will warm you up."

They both drank in silence, a bit shy, not knowing what to say.

Catherine asked Bidzill a few questions about his life in the Indian village during winter. Bidzill answered shyly at first and, after a while, more confidently, warming up to Catherine's kindness.

"In the winter," he continued, "us men, we make stone and wooden utensils and tools; we also repair the village structures if needed. We make canoes for our fishing trips, pipes, snowshoes and sledges."

"You are really busy," exclaimed Catherine. "Just like us," she answered, smiling. "Your French is so good now," she says. "Congratulations!"

"I have a good teacher," he replies, smiling at Marie. "I

must get back to my village; it is getting dark," says Bidzill sadly, looking at Marie.

"It was very nice to meet you, Bidzill," Catherine adds.

Marie and Bidzill go outside and chat for a little while. "I will come back and see you," he says.

"I hope to return to your village and see you again as soon as the snow starts melting," she answers. They smile at each other, and Marie watches him leave, impatient to see him again soon.

Antoine and Marguerite are delighted to see Joseph's daily progress; he can now sit, smile, giggle and respond well by gurgling to his parents' words. "He is so clever he'll be walking, and he will start speaking by the time I come back late summer!" says Antoine.

What a proud and loving father he is, thought Marguerite.

As Pierre and Catherine were due to marry at the end of April, Pierre decided that Marguerite and Antoine could move to his farmhouse as it was more spacious than the first house they had as a wedding present.

Pierre was ready to move in with Catherine and help her with her farm and the boys.

Pierre still had feelings for Marguerite but felt it was time to move on. Marguerite was married to his best friend and was a mother now. He liked Catherine and her boys very much and wanted to start his own family.

February and March were by far the busiest months for both couples.

Antoine and Marguerite had packed all their belongings to move to their new home, La Source. They were delighted to have more space. There was an extra bedroom so Joseph could have his own room.

The storage room was also quite big, so it would enable them to store more food next winter. Marguerite and Antoine had a small garden in their first house, allowing them to grow a few vegetables. Pierre's farming land, on the other hand, was much more extensive and kept Antoine very busy. Marguerite thought farming would be overwhelming and daunting when Antoine was away. Fortunately, both Pierre and Catherine's farm hands said they would help, especially now she was expecting another baby, and Pierre was staying with Catherine. Antoine reassured her that all the seeding and planting would be done before his departure. Hopefully, he would be back for the harvest in the autumn.

Pierre had now moved in with Catherine. After adjusting to a new routine for a few days, he felt really at home and loved having the boys around. It was everything he wished for: a big family after being so lonely. Catherine was an excellent companion for him. He thought she was fun, kind, and able to help manage the farm. Both were making preparations for their wedding. It would be a small affair as Catherine had been married before. Just a trip to the church and a small celebration with their friends. The boys were getting quite excited about it, particularly the younger ones. Catherine and Pierre had involved them in the preparations, and Catherine's eldest, Philippe, was asked to read a passage from the bible in the church. He was very proud to oblige. "I am the man in charge," he told everyone proudly.

Meantime, Marie had started going back to the Indian village. The snow had started melting, and her journey there was much more manageable.

Apart from continuing to teach Bidzill, she had started teaching French to some Indian children and teenagers once a week. The nuns and the Indian chief had agreed it would benefit the two communities, though both had different agendas. The nuns were hoping to convert the Indian community to Christianity, particularly the children. In contrast, the Indian chief thought it would improve trade if more of them spoke French.

Marie knew this but didn't care as long as she could see Bidzill as often as possible. She had become very popular in the Indian village. The children loved her patience and fun way of teaching, and she always stayed longer after tutoring to play little games with them. She liked the time she spent speaking to the elders as she could now converse with the Huron quite fluently. She quickly embraced their lifestyle and was showered with presents such as beads, jewellery, beautiful Indian clothing and moccasins.

She had even agreed to have her hair plaited by one of the Indian women.

Bidzill was very proud of her, and it was not long before he asked his father if he could marry her. Marie, of course, knew of his intentions, and it was all she wanted. His father said he would consult with the elders and let him know during the next full moon, which was two weeks away.

The next step for Marie was to talk to her sister and Catherine and, of course, to the nuns. She was almost sure she would get approval from her sister and Catherine as both knew how happy she was with Bidzill; however, convincing the priest and the nuns was another matter. She knew the reverse was quite acceptable in the name of Christianity. Still, a French woman marrying an Indian boy was another matter, especially when there was a shortage of women for French settlers in Quebec.

April came, and on the fifteenth, Catherine and Pierre celebrated their marriage. They enjoyed a small celebration with their friends and Catherine's boys.

Marguerite and Antoine were very happy for them and delighted to have moved to Pierre's bigger house. Pierre had gifted the house to them, provided he could still work some of the big patches of land surrounding it.

Antoine was preparing to leave again for the hunting and fishing summer season. Marguerite was getting anxious and worried about it as she always had Pierre around to help when Antoine was away. Now Pierre had moved in with Catherine, she worried she would feel a bit lonely, especially as Catherine's farm was a bit of a distance to go to with a young toddler.

Catherine and Pierre kept reassuring her that they would come and help regularly. Catherine offered to send her the two farm workers if needed.

Antoine comforted Marguerite. "My love, you are in good hands with good friends," he told her and left in May, hoping to return at the summer's end.

6

Happiness and sorrow

Summer arrived, and again, everyone was busy. Marguerite was just a few weeks away from giving birth, so Catherine, Antoine and the two farm hands came regularly to help at La Source farm.

Marie also was helping Marguerite a lot, looking after little Joseph to give her sister a rest. She had, in fact, moved into La Source after Catherine and Pierre's wedding.

Marie was spending most of her days at the Indian village or at the orphanage teaching. Still, Marguerite was delighted to spend the evenings with her. She loved her sister's company and support, and Marie loved little Joseph. He was a lovely child. He smiled and made gurgling noises; Marguerite was adamant he was already saying "*maman*"!

He was very active and crawled constantly; it would not be long before he could walk. *His father will be so proud*, thought Marguerite. In the evening Marie talked a lot about the Indian village and how happy she was there.

Some native women had taught her to recognise the plants and trees used to cure various diseases.

"Do you know they use different parts of the pine trees for various ailments? For example, they make tea with the bark or branches for sore throats, coughs and colds. They have recipes to help with digestive problems, headaches, respiratory difficulties and many more. I am still learning so much!" she said enthusiastically.

She also confided to Marguerite that the chief was very fond of her, and Bidzill was waiting to hear from his father and the elders.

Would they agree for her and Bidzill to marry?

If they agreed, she would then consult the priest and the nuns. She did not need their approval but was keen not to become an outcast with the French settlers. Quebec was such a devoted small Catholic community where everyone knew everyone's business. She also wanted to keep her teaching and her job as a translator and interpreter at the convent; it was also bringing her a small income and standing in the community. Marie was well respected and admired for her dedication.

Marguerite was really happy for Marie, but now the role was reversed; she was anxious to find herself alone if Marie was to marry when Antoine was away for so long.

July arrived, and on the twenty-seventh Marguerite gave birth to a beautiful little girl. She called her Antoinette after her father. She thought Antoine would be proud and delighted on his return. The delivery went well, and the baby weighed three kilograms, which was quite a lot.

She had her mum's beautiful eyes and hair. Everyone fussed over Marguerite and Antoinette, helping around doing chores and bringing food. Marguerite seemed very cheerful the first few days, doting on her daughter. Joseph was curious and intrigued about this new baby, a bit jealous at first but warming to her.

Joseph was walking now, and it was almost a full-time job keeping an eye on him. He was an active toddler full of mischief. Every now and then, he would come and put his finger on his sister's cheeks, saying "Net-Net", not able yet to pronounce her full name but trying.

A week or so after Antoinette's birth, her friend and Marie noticed that Marguerite was getting very quiet, not speaking much, becoming overprotective and fussing over her children. *Her behaviour is odd*, thought Pierre and Catherine, who checked on her every day when Marie was working.

Marguerite became relentlessly obsessive, asking herself, "Am I a good mother? I am so tired all the time I feel I cannot cope, and sometimes I feel uncontrollably resentful."

Depression was setting in again, and she wanted to hide her feelings. She was missing Antoine so much. *Where was he?* she wondered.

It was like black clouds and fog in her mind again. She was feeling so hopeless. *Now I have a daughter, will I be able to protect her?* Awful and upsetting memories flooded her mind. Her mother was a good person but could not save her from her father's abuse. Marguerite started crying and felt so alone and powerless, just as she felt when she was a little girl. Her father would go into her bed, putting his hand on her mouth, threatening to kill her if she screamed or talked. He would force her into indescribable sexual acts from the age of seven. She felt so sick when he would push his penis in her mouth and, from age eight, penetrated her savagely almost every night. Marguerite was raped repeatedly.

She never told anyone. Who would listen to her? Becoming oblivious to the physical and mental pain he inflicted on her, she believed all the shame was her shame, her fault. How could she protect her little girl in the future from horrible men like her father? She knew her thoughts were unreasonable just now; after all, she was a married woman with a good husband and friends in the community, a new life. She could not help, however, to be haunted by her past.

It was mid-August when Antoine came back. For the first few days of his return, everyone was rejoicing. He was so happy to see his new daughter and son. Even Marguerite started to smile again. The hunt and fishing had been good for Antoine, and the harvest was one of the best Catherine and Pierre had ever seen since arriving in Quebec.

Marie was also thrilled. The father of Bidzill and the elders had agreed to their marriage. The priest and nuns initially opposed it but decided it could be advantageous to convert more indigenous people to Christianity with Marie's help by being part of the Huron community. They insisted, however, that after their marriage in the Indian community, there should also be a ceremony in the church. Bidzill had agreed to get baptised to become a Catholic, so the wedding could occur.

Marie and Bidzill married at the end of August, first in the church and then had another ceremony in her Indian village.

The wedding was a success, and Marie and Bidzill seemed to love each other very much.

Marguerite and her family, Pierre and Catherine, and friends participated in the wedding festivities. They were made to feel so welcome by the Indian community that they agreed to be firm friends from now on and have closer trading ties; the men smoked together and laughed, drinking the local brew they called "*Eau de Feu*", or fire water. The festivities were joyous and lively. All the Indian ladies were wearing their traditional party dresses and beads, and there was a lot of dancing and cheering.

Marie would live in the Indian community from now on, and she was pleased about it. She had embraced their way of life and customs. The new bride loved belonging to a real community, people helping each other and very inclusive of children and elders. It was very different from her life in France, where she felt that only her sister truthfully cared and looked after her.

She had been asked to continue her teaching work with the nuns, and she had accepted, rejoicing at the idea that it would allow her to see Marguerite regularly. Her workplace was close to Marguerite's farm, and she could see her sister and the children most days.

Marguerite was a bit apprehensive about Marie joining the Indian community. Still, most of all, she wanted Marie to be happy, and Marie's life seemed to be so fulfilled with Bidzill.

Marguerite was still anxious, as she felt Antoine had changed after his return. He was becoming more distant towards her and snapped at her and the children quite a lot. "Can't you keep that baby quiet! She is always crying!"

After a while, he started to be restless; he did not seem interested in his daughter and mainly devoted all his time and attention to Joseph.

"Soon, my son, I will take you hunting and fishing with me; we'll make a great team." Joseph had just started to speak and was looking at his dad, full of admiration.

Antoine also started telling Marguerite, "Snap out of your misery! I am fed up seeing your sour face! There is so much a man can take!"

Instead of cheering her up, it was really getting her down. Antoine had never been so unsupportive and dismissive of her before. Marguerite felt worthless and so guilty that she made Antoine cross with her; it was all her fault for not being a good mother and wife.

There was a pattern of blaming herself. Her self-esteem was so low.

Only three weeks after the wedding of Marie and Bidzill, Antoine announced that he was going back to France for a few months and would be back in the spring. He made his announcement when all his close friends and family were around.

"What?" said Marguerite, aghast. "You are leaving us for the winter. Why?"

"Why?" asked Pierre and Marie in unison, looking concerned.

"Firstly, I want to see my mother again, my father died last year and she is alone. Also, I am planning to go to Paris to sell directly the furs we caught this hunting year; I will get at least ten times the price I would sell them for here," said Antoine with a determination in his eyes, which scared Marguerite.

"You cannot leave Marguerite and the children on their own for the winter; you need to be here to help," answered Pierre crossly, adding, "you never cared for your mother much before, and the sale of the furs here in Quebec gives you a decent life and some decent earnings!"

Antoine hesitated, seeing everyone around him looking angry, and answered back.

"I won't go for long, and I'll be back with many luxuries for you all! Besides, you have been such good friends helping Marguerite when I am away; a bit longer won't hurt."

Marie, who knew how depressed Marguerite was already, shouted at him. "You just cannot leave now; it will be too much hardship for my sister; she will be alone, looking after two young children all winter!"

"My mind is made up. I am leaving on the next boat for La Rochelle on Thursday next week," he said coldly and stormed outside.

Everyone was stunned by his behaviour, and Marguerite started crying, comforted by Marie and

Catherine. No one could believe he had booked his trip back to France without talking to Marguerite first.

It was half an hour later when Antoine reappeared. He seemed to have cooled down; he apologised to everyone, took Marguerite in his arms and kissed her tenderly to appease her. "Listen," he said gently, "I won't be long, just a few months to trade the furs. I'll be back in no time on the next spring crossing available, and I'll get someone to write so you will hear from me."

The few days before his departure, Antoine's behaviour improved, and he became more supportive and kinder to Marguerite and the children. He did all he could to ensure a good winter supply of wood and food. Dry fish and cured games were plentiful in the pantry. He played with the children and was delighted at his baby daughter's first smiles. He managed to get Marguerite smiling again as his good mood and fun was contagious. He was again the wonderful man she fell in love with. Thursday arrived, and Antoine was ready to leave early in the morning. Marguerite, the children, and Marie went to the harbour to say goodbye. Marguerite and Joseph were crying, begging him to come back soon. "You are all so dear to me." He kissed them and walked away. "I'll try to be back as soon as possible," he shouted as he waved. The horn of the ship blasted, and the boat heading for France left on a foggy late-September day before the ice took hold of the St. Lawrence.

7

A DIFFICULT WINTER

Marguerite went back home, comforting the children, telling them their father would be back soon, trying to reassure herself as well. She knew he would not return before the spring once the ice melted on the river St. Lawrence, allowing the boats to navigate and enter the harbour.

Meanwhile, Catherine and Pierre were expecting their first child and were both so happy about it. Catherine's boys were also delighted at the news, and secretly, Catherine and her boys hoped it would be a baby girl. The baby was due in April, and already everyone was telling Catherine to take it easy and rest. She would laugh about all this fussing and say, "I already gave birth to five boys! I'll surely manage another birth."

Pierre felt very happy and settled with Catherine; he loved her boys. Catherine was a robust, reliable and delightful woman. She was also a good mother, and a child of their own would complete the family.

Pierre felt very fortunate to have found a good woman.

Occasionally, his feelings for Marguerite would emerge, and he felt so sad for her. He was still very angry with Antoine for leaving his family at this time of the year but hoped he would be back soon.

Marie and Bidzill were also very content. They helped and supported each other all the time. The love between them was for everyone to see. The chief was very proud of his son.

Bidzill had become more confident and physically stronger; he commanded respect and admiration among his tribe. He was given more responsibilities and led a group of men for the hunts. His French was now fluent, thanks to Marie's teaching, and soon, he would also be in charge of trading with the French.

Marie still enjoyed teaching at the convent. Her reputation as an effective and competent teacher was spreading, and a few prominent families in Quebec wanted her to tutor their children privately. She only accepted a couple of offers as it helped her financially, but her life was already so busy.

She was also very keen to keep learning about medicine. She read a lot, borrowing books from the convent's library. She was particularly interested in childbirth as so many women and babies died in childbirth in Quebec. One of the nuns, Bernadette, assisted with many birth deliveries, and Marie asked her many questions while taking notes. She also asked Sister Bernadette if she could come with her and help one day. In the meantime, Marie continued her medical learning with the Hurons ladies; they had excellent knowledge about many plants to cure or relieve pain. Marie felt great respect for them.

They dealt with witchcraft and sorcery, using drugs and herbal remedies to help the sick, and sometimes, they used masks and shells to conjure evil spirits.

These Huron ladies were highly paid and respected for their role and wisdom in the community.

What appealed to Marie about the Huron society was that it was a monogamous tribe, and marriage could be terminated by either party at any time. It was so different from the French rules. French married women were entirely at the mercy and goodwill of their husbands financially and in every other aspect of their lives. Once married, they could not leave. A man was in charge and had all the rights of the law on his side.

She thought about Antoine, who left Marguerite for the winter without discussing it with her beforehand, and she had no say in it. This infuriated Marie. She thought, *I will never let a man do that to me!*

Marie kept seeing Marguerite twice a week to keep an eye on her sister's well-being. It was almost two months since Antoine's departure, and Marguerite seemed to be doing well. She had received many orders for ball gowns and hats and met many ladies coming in and out for their dress fittings. It kept her busy and her mind off Antoine. Catherine and Pierre visited her regularly with their boys, and sometimes, she would go to them with Joseph and Antoinette for dinner.

Catherine's boys were very good at playing and entertaining Joseph. Joseph loved it as he was the centre of attention. He was a real character, good-natured and funny. His speech was coming on well. He was learning new words every day. "Pipi, caca" was its latest antic to make the boys laugh. He could have a few tantrums, but it didn't last. Antoinette sat in her pram watching everyone, smiling; she was a real gem, a placid and easy baby. Everyone admired her gentle nature.

"I want a baby sister like Toinette," said Robert one day. As one of the youngest of Catherine's children, he was the first to express his preference loudly! Everyone laughed.

Marguerite was delighted when she heard that Catherine and Pierre were expecting a baby. She was very supportive of Catherine, in particular, knowing how hard it had been for her after the passing of her son Nicolas. Catherine had also asked Marguerite to be the godmother of the forthcoming baby, and Marguerite thought it was a great honour.

In no time, Christmas arrived, and every family was getting ready to celebrate. At this time of the year, there were a lot of church activities. There were a lot of Masses to celebrate the birth of Christ and religious singing in the church. Many parcels and food were provided to ensure no one would go hungry at this time of the year. Plenty of blankets and clothes were distributed to the community's poorest members. It was really the season of goodwill, and it was so comforting to see everyone helping each other during the coldest and hardest season.

The nuns had also set up a drop-in free surgery in the convent to help the sick. Many people at this time of the year were getting colds, flu and other infections due to the freezing temperatures. Marie was also involved in helping and took great pride in it.

She encouraged some Hurons in her community to come along, particularly the women, the children and the elders. European settlers had brought their viruses over to Quebec and unwittingly infected Indian communities with less immunity against new viruses such as cold and flu. Already, four elderly people had died from the cold virus among the Huron tribe. Two young Indian boys were also suffering from an ear infection. Marie had urged the mothers to bring the children to the surgery. The nuns had remedies to help them. The Indian community already knew about medicinal plants, but new diseases are now affecting them. The arrival of French settlers had been a disaster for indigenous tribes.

Christmas Day arrived, and Pierre and Catherine invited their friends around, cooking a big meal to celebrate. Marie and Bidzill, Marguerite, her children, and the two farm hands came along. The food was plentiful, with venison, fish, fresh bread, and homemade cakes. Marie and Bidzill had brought a present for each of the children.

The Indian men and women from the Huron community had been busy making a present for each child. For the boys, they made some beautiful wooden carvings of the various wild animals living around Quebec: bears, wolves, eagles, moose, foxes, deer and beavers. The boys were delighted; the eldest, Philippe, was given the bear as he was the tallest and oldest. Baptiste received the wolf carving as he was the quickest on his feet. Robert, who was almost seven, got the eagle as he was known to love birds. The youngest, Paul, received the beaver carving, which was supposed to bring good luck and provide him with good hunting skills. Joseph was given a fish to enhance his future skills as a fisherman.

Bidzill had been instrumental regarding the choice of presents for the boys. He had gotten to know each of them. He observed them over the time he spent with Marie and tried to find, according to Indian traditions, an animal suited to each of them.

Bidzill was hesitant about what to give Antoinette because she was still so young, so he had asked his sisters and mother for some advice.

They decided to make a small Indian doll for her with colourful clothes and beads. Six months old, Antoinette was beaming with joy when she saw it, and she grabbed it, probably attracted by the colourful beads.

It was a very joyful moment, and the celebrations lasted well into the night. The two farm hands, Jacques and Francois, fell asleep at the table. They were getting older, and all the food and drinks provided that evening rendered them oblivious to all the noises the children were making. The older children kept running around the table with their animal carvings, chasing each other to entertain Joseph and Antoinette and make them laugh.

Each boy was trying to make the sound the animal was supposed to make! It was an absolute cacophony, but all the adults thought it was great to hear and see so much fun and happiness. *It is a day to enjoy and cherish*, thought Marie.

She was so proud of Bidzill for being so thoughtful. She told him that, and he turned to her lovingly and said, "I am so looking forward for us to have a family."

She smiled back and answered: "Me too, but not just yet."

She was looking forward to having children, but at the moment, she was enjoying her busy and exciting life. She was a bit anxious about all the changes having children might bring. She did not see herself as a stay-at-home mother; would it be expected of her as it was from most married women?

The Christmas period had been a hectic and joyful time for everyone; it was now January, and everyone was settling down again to their daily routine. It was an unusually freezing winter with a bad snowstorm and a nasty blizzard lasting over two weeks. It meant that many people were stuck at home. It was past mid-January when Marie finally was able to go back to teaching at the convent and revisit her sister Marguerite.

Marie was aghast when she visited Marguerite late afternoon for the first time since Christmas. Marguerite had lost weight and had a vacant look on her face; the house was a mess, very unlike Marguerite, who always had been so house-proud. The children were fine but looking a bit sad. Joseph ran to Marie when she arrived and wrapped his arms around her waist. "Tata Marie," he shouted with a big smile, "come play with me." He had the wood carving fish he had received for Christmas in his hand.

He seemed so happy to see her. It was heartbreaking. She turned around and saw Antoinette sitting on a blanket, reaching out to her to be carried. Marguerite had hardly registered her sister's visit, looking at her with a haggard face and dark skin under her eyes.

"How are you? What's wrong?" asked Marie to her sister.

"Nothing," answered Marguerite unconvincingly.

"Speak to me," said Marie. "You look so unwell; what's the matter?"

Marguerite stayed silent for a while and said, "Antoine is never coming home. Is he? I am so lonely."

"Have you heard from him? How do you know?" Marie asked.

Marguerite took a few minutes to answer. "No, I have no news. He forgot about us; I just know I am not worthy of him; he is too good for me!"

Marie saw red. "You must be kidding; you're lovely and an exceptional human being. He is the one who doesn't deserve you; you gave him two beautiful children, and he goes back to France when you most need him." Adding: "He'll be back in the spring anyway, when boats are doing the crossing again, remember the St. Lawrence is blocked by ice until March," realising her sister needed cheering up.

Marguerite answered with a hopeful look, "Do you think so?"

Then, she was silent again.

Marie played with the children and cooked some dinner for them. The weather was so bad at this time of the year that Marie had planned to stay for three nights with her sister while working at the convent during the day. Bidzill was going to pick her up with his sledge on Thursday afternoon. After the third evening spent with Marguerite and the children, Marie was seriously concerned about her sister's state of mind. Marguerite hardly ate or communicated; she cared for her children but barely spoke or played with them. She went through the motions of feeding the children and dressing them up, making sure they were kept clean. Still, apart from looking after the children, she did no housework or other tasks.

Her dressmaking had dried up in January because all the Christmas festivities were over. Still, she had not taken any other requests from customers wanting new hats or children's clothes. Marie was heartbroken to see Marguerite in such a sorry state and totally irresponsive to any help or suggestions.

When Bidzill came to pick her up on Thursday to go back to the Indian village, Marie went back with a heavy heart. She talked to him about her worries.

"What am I going to do?" she told him. "I am worried about her but also about the children; she seems so absent and distant. She is losing her mind."

After giving it some thought, Bidzill was a caring and wise young man and answered: "I think she should move to our village for a while; she and the children would be well looked after by our community, she would never be alone, and Joseph and Antoinette could play and mix with the other children."

Marie looked at him gratefully. "That would be wonderful, Bidzill, and it would put my mind at rest to know they are safe with the community keeping an eye on them."

Bidzill smiles at her and reassuringly says, "Don't worry, my Elu, I'll speak to my father and the elders tonight to get their approval; I am sure it will be fine."

The elders all agreed it would be better for Marguerite and the children to move to the Indian village. They had consulted the whole community, asking for the women's and the men's consent before making their final decision. The community was so fond of Marie that they were all looking forward to having her family living among them, even if it was for a short time.

The week after, Bidzill and Marie went to pick up Marguerite and the children. Marguerite was a bit bewildered, not quite sure of what was happening.

"Pack up; you are moving with us to our village until Antoine's return. I am worried about your health. You need help being on your own with the children," said Marie firmly. Marguerite started packing silently with Marie's help. Marguerite did not know what to say or feel about moving; she felt so low and helpless that she was somehow relieved someone else was thinking for her. She did not seem to care one way or another about what was happening to her.

When they arrived at the Indian camp, Bidzill and Marie settled Marguerite and the children next to their own quarters. They wanted to keep a close eye on Marguerite.

Everything was ready; the villagers had kindly prepared a comfortable space for them next to Marie and Bidzill's quarters. The children sounded happy to see new faces as their mother's sombre mood had made them sad and concerned. They had picked up on their mother's low spirit without knowing what was wrong.

Many Indian women and children came to welcome them and brought little homemade presents. Joseph and little Antoinette were delighted to see other children. The whole community had prepared a special meal to share with them.

Marguerite appeared to be more settled and active with the children over the next few days. When Marie was working, teaching at the convent, the women made sure Marguerite was never alone and, as they knew Marguerite was a good seamstress, they started to bring her cloth and thread, asking her to teach them some of her skills and showed her in return the type of clothes and sewing they did themselves.

Language was a problem as they needed to understand each other. Still, both the women and Marguerite tried to learn a few words from their respective languages.

Joseph was really enjoying being there. He was playing with the other children every day. After three weeks with the Huron community, he understood and communicated reasonably well with the native children.

Antoinette was also blooming as everyone was fussing around her. She was such a pretty and placid little girl; she, too, began picking words and learning the local language.

Marie was still concerned about Marguerite. She

seemed slightly happier here but hardly spoke to anyone much, including her and the children. She was, in fact, worried that the children would forget their French, so she made sure to speak French to them every day when she came back from work.

In winter, it was also a busy time for the men. Bidzill and his men kept busy mainly ice fishing and storing the fish, while some of the other men in the tribe made stones and wooden utensils and tools. All the activities fascinated Joseph, and he kept pestering Bidzill to take him fishing. "You are too young, Joseph, you can come when you're a bit older, promise!"

There was so much to do in the winter. Some of the village structures needed repairing, and things such as snowshoes, sledges, pipes and especially canoes demanded to be made or repaired before the spring.

Catherine and Pierre visited their friends a few times as they were worried about Marguerite; she was a shadow of herself, having lost so much weight and unable to sustain a conversation anymore. What was going on in that head of hers?

Marguerite had reached a point where she was unable to function. All she could think was: *I am a bad mother, I am a bad wife, that's why Antoine left me; I am not worthy of him.*

She tormented herself with the past, her secret, her father's shadow being a constant reminder. She felt unclean and worthless and was too ashamed to confide in anyone. She even convinced herself it was all her fault for attracting her father's attention. She felt impure and unworthy of anyone.

Her moods and behaviour once again became so erratic that everyone in the village became worried without knowing what to do to help her.

The medicine lady concocted an herbal tea for her to try to uplift her mood, but she refused to drink it. Nothing seemed to help or have any effect on her. Everyone was worried because she was hardly eating anything and was in a permanent state of melancholy.

Luckily, the children were so well looked after in the village and so happy to play with other children that they just accepted Maman as she was, kissing her on the cheek before being put to bed by Marie and Bidzill. Both were reassured to see the children joyful, unaware of their mother's depression. Joseph and Antoinette were too young to realise their mother's illness. *Children are very resilient*, thought Marie, remembering she and her sister spent much of their childhood in the orphanage.

However, Marie felt very upset and helpless about Marguerite not getting better.

She realised that she should maybe send a letter to Antoine to let him know and ask him to come back as soon as possible. She was not sure though, she did not have much faith in him. Why did he leave his family behind? It was such a selfish and callous action! Did he have any intention of coming back? Perhaps he just said he would be back to stop everyone from being so angry with him?

It was the end of February, and by mid-March,

boats would be running again, that is, if the ice in the St. Lawrence was clearing.

Let's hope he comes back soon, she prayed.

On the morning of the third of March, Marie heard Antoinette crying. She noticed Marguerite was not sleeping next to her children. Marie had an awful feeling but tried to put it out of her mind. It was early, and she wondered where Marguerite was.

She called Bidzill and asked him to come with her and look for her sister. Most of the villagers were still asleep on this cold winter morning. Bidzill and Marie walked around the village hoping to find her nearby, but no sign of Marguerite. She could not be far away. *It is so difficult to walk in so much snow*, Marie thought. The village was surrounded by woods, so knowing which direction to follow was hard. This was rendered more treacherous as it was snowing again, and they could not see any shoe tracks on the ground to get a lead. Firstly, they walked south, thinking that Marguerite, in her absent state, perhaps wanted to get back home to La Source.

After walking in that direction for thirty minutes, they realised there was no indication she had walked there. As the snowfall was worsening, they decided to turn back and organise a search party to look for her.

"What was she thinking going out on her own in such bad weather!" cried Marie, trying to comfort herself."

"She probably went for a short walk to clear her head and got lost," added Bidzill. She was so concerned about her sister's low spirits lately that she did not know what to think.

All the men in the village started to look for her. They organised themselves into groups in order to explore different directions around the camp. It was nine o'clock in the morning when all the groups began their search, but it was foggy, and finding her would be a challenge. At one o'clock most of them came back with a beaten look, no sign of Marguerite. It was bitterly cold for the beginning of March, still minus ten, when they started their search. Everyone was concerned if she was lost in the forest, would she survive in such cold weather.

She was wearing her heavy winter coat, but would it be enough? Nobody thought so. Perhaps she reached her home farm, and she is now warm and safe, but it was doubtful as none of the sledges or carriages was missing; there was no way she could reach her farm on foot. Bidzill and Marie, however, decided to get the sledge out and check if she was back there.

There was no sign of Marguerite when they reached La Source farm. They decided to go to Les Eaux Vives to see if she was at Catherine's farm. Unfortunately, Marguerite was not there, and when Pierre was told that Marguerite could not be found, he had a terrible feeling about her disappearance and was devastated, thinking the worst. He called Catherine, who was now heavily pregnant, and told her the news; she burst into tears, feeling desperately helpless.

She told Pierre, "Please go with them and see if you can find her." The three of them left as a last attempt to find Marguerite, but their mood was dark, and they were losing hope. The night was falling by the time they arrived home.

The following day, the snowfall had stopped, and it was sunny. The search for Marguerite started again. It was late morning when a small group of three Hurons men discovered Marguerite not far from the village. Her body was frozen, crouching under a tree half covered by snow; her lips were blue, and her hands were clutched together as if she had been praying. They carried her body back to the village. When Marie saw her sister's body, she screamed, "Why?" She was so distraught to lose her beloved Marguerite. What was she going to tell the children?

Before taking Marguerite's body back to Quebec City Church for burial, Marie had agreed with Bidzill to tell the priest and nuns that Marguerite's death was an accident and that she got lost after her late afternoon walk around the village. Marguerite knew her sister had given up the will to live, but for the Catholic Church, it was a sin to let yourself give up on life, and she wanted her sister to have a Christian burial. Marie was crying her eyes out when she removed the little cross around Marguerite's neck; she knew it was her sister's wish to pass it on to her daughter Antoinette one day. How could such a beautiful young and talented girl like Marguerite have such a tragic end?

Marie knew her sister had died of a broken heart with Antoine leaving her for so long; she felt so angry with him that there were no words for her pain and fury.

8

Funeral and new birth

Three days after her death, Marguerite's funeral took place. It was a very sad day. The whole Indian community and all her friends attended the church service. She was buried in the cemetery behind the church. Marie was holding Joseph's hand and Bidzill was carrying Antoinette. Everyone threw a bit of earth on the coffin before the burial.

Marie had explained to Joseph that his mother had gone on a long trip. Joseph did not quite understand what was going on as he was now almost three years old. He cried briefly and said, "Maman is going away to see Papa."

Marie just said, "*Oui.*" She left it at that as he was too young to understand.

The whole village rallied around Marie and Bidzill. "Don't worry, we'll look after the children as if they were our own," they said. She was so grateful for their support and for the fact she could continue her work during the day. She loved her nephew and her niece and took comfort she could see them every day and look after them as much as possible. It was a way of keeping Marguerite's memory alive and it was important to her. She had also promised the nuns she would bring them to the convent regularly for them to get a religious education once they were a bit older.

Marie also wrote a letter to Antoine to the address of his friend in Paris to let him know about Marguerite's death. It probably would take a while to reach him as the boats were not sailing at this time of the year. She wondered, *does Antoine have any intention of coming back anyway?*

She really had her doubts. She did not trust his motives for leaving in the first place.

Pierre was badly affected by Marguerite's death. He felt as a friend he had failed her. Busy with his own family and work life, he blamed himself for not checking on her more often. He knew how vulnerable she was after Pierre's departure.

Catherine tried to comfort him. "It is not your fault. Antoine should have been here for her." He knew she was right but he always had such strong feelings for Marguerite that he could not help his sadness and guilt.

Most days after the funeral he went to Marguerite's grave and talked to her. Often crying and apologising for letting her down, telling her how much he loved her from the first time he saw her walking off the boat. His love for her was his secret and he felt somehow better after saying it loud on her grave. She never knew as he was such a gentleman and it had been enough for him to know she was happy with Antoine. When he thought of Antoine, he felt enraged. He should have been firm with him and forced him to stay. Pierre also felt guilty because he knew Antoine had not been a reliable character in the past. He was a bit of a womaniser, leaving many broken-hearted girls in France. He thought though that when he married Marguerite and with two beautiful children he had changed.

After Marguerite's death Pierre had decided to lease his farm, La Source, to a young couple who wanted to settle in Quebec and start a family. He knew now that Antoine was not coming back and decided with Catherine that the money from the lease would be saved for Marguerite's children Joseph and Antoinette until they were old enough to manage the farm themselves if they wished.

The weather was improving and Pierre thought it was time to initiate Catherine's two eldest boys to hunting and trapping. Philippe was thirteen now and Baptiste almost twelve. The boys were very excited about it and Pierre thought it would give Catherine some peace and quiet before the birth of their first child.

He explained to the boys that trapping was used in order to avoid damaging the animal's fur. The furs could be sold at a good price or used to make clothing or shoes. They first went in the forest and Pierre showed the boys how to set traps for catching foxes, later they walked back towards the banks of the river and they put out a couple of traps to catch a beaver. Beaver pelts were particularly valuable because there was a lot of demand for them. The boys were very hopeful and excited! "We'll come back in a few days and see if we have caught anything," said Pierre. They all went home for supper, the boys beaming and proud and told Catherine all about their day.

She smiled. "You'll soon be young men, my sons, and in no time, you will be able to help Pierre run the farm."

Both boys were keen to learn about farming and hunting. However, Baptiste seemed to be the one who had more aptitude for practical tasks. He had really struggled to learn to read and still now his reading skills were poor but he was a wizard when it came time to build, to sow, to harvest and to fish. He picked up all his skills by watching others and he was a very fast learner. Pierre and Marguerite had been so impressed last year when he built four wooden stools for the kitchen from his own initiative.

The eldest Philippe was completely different: of a gentle temperament and more academic. He had been an excellent student and Marie had taught him so much. He could read and write very well and was also good with arithmetic. He also spent time with his younger siblings teaching them to read once Marie had not been able to come and do it anymore.

Two days later Pierre and the boys went back to the areas where they had set up traps. In the forest most traps were empty bare one. "It's a fox," shouted Philippe. "We caught a fox!" he repeated. The boys were so proud they would have something to bring back home to their mother. They did not find anything else near the river, it was much more difficult to catch beavers. After all, it was their first hunting experience.

"You will learn a bit more each time we go," said Pierre to them. "Tt is a skill which takes time to master," he concluded, smiling at the boys.

They went home tired but happy. Philippe and Baptiste felt a sense of achievement. They were keen to help Pierre and Catherine especially with the forthcoming birth. Pierre was happy too. He was very fond of the boys and got on well with them. He had no regrets about marrying Catherine, she was such a wise person and a good mother and he felt a special kind of love for her, he was so proud she was his wife. Every night once they were lying in bed, he loved touching her round belly, feeling the baby, his baby moving and kicking. He would kiss his wife's belly gently and then embrace Catherine in his arms, telling her how happy he was with her.

As a surprise for Baptiste's birthday in May, Pierre was planning to show the two boys how to build a small canoe called commonly "*canot batard*". It would allow them to penetrate small streams to go fishing. The bark of large paper birch trees was used and stretched over a white cedar frame. This was quite a skilled undertaking but Pierre was confident he would be able to build it as he had some joinery skills and had built a couple of them in the past.

The weather was getting better now. Tt was the beginning of April, the snow was melting, making an awful mess of puddles and mud on pathways, but it was sunny and it was definitely getting warmer. The trees were budding and you could see some plant growths timidly coming out of the ground.

It was in the morning of the sixteenth of April that Catherine suddenly went into labour. She was preparing lunch in the kitchen when her waters broke. After having five babies she knew exactly what was happening. She told Philippe to go and fetch Pierre and Baptiste who were working outdoors and she told her two younger boys to get some warm, clean water and clean towels. She went to her bedroom and laid on the bed getting ready to push. Pierre arrived in a panic. It was his first child and he had never assisted a woman giving birth. Catherine stayed calm and told Pierre what to do. She encouraged him to help her while she was pushing the baby out of her womb. "You are doing well," she told him reassuringly, seeing his worried expression.

Pierre saw the top of a head and started to pull gently, and in no time the baby came out and cried. "It's a girl!" said Pierre with tears in his eyes. After cutting the umbilical cord, he placed her gently in Catherine's arms and kissed both of them.

It was not long after that the boys came to see their baby sister. "This is your new baby sister 'Marguerite'," said Pierre proudly.

The boys wanted to kiss her and touch her but Catherine said, smiling, "Just wait a day or two, until she settles."

She thought it would be too overwhelming for little

Marguerite to have the boys here one after the other wanting to carry her and making a big fuss.

"Give your mother a rest now, us boys will go and get some dinner," Pierre said gently.

The all family was over the moon. "Mother and baby were doing well," confirmed the doctor and the nun who came to check on Catherine after the birth.

When Marie and Bidzill heard the news of the birth they were delighted and came over to see the baby the following Sunday after church.

Marie was so touched that Pierre and Catherine had decided to name the baby after her sister. It was like a new beginning.

Marie missed Marguerite terribly but life went on and for the sake of her nephew and niece she had to be strong. Catherine had now asked Marie to be baby Marguerite's godmother. Marie was delighted and thought she would cherish that little girl bearing her dear sister's name.

It was now the end of April and the boats coming from France were doing the crossing.

Marie thought, *Antoine is never coming back otherwise he would be here by now.*

She suddenly felt great sadness for the children he abandoned and at the same time she was so angry with his callous behaviour that had caused so much pain and the death of her sister.

The celebration was short-lived as Quebec started to suffer a terrible new epidemic of "*fievre pourpre*", which was a form of typhus.

April had brought warmer weather and the winter's biting cold had faded. At this time of the year unfortunately the melting of the snow, as usual, turned the ground into a quagmire of puddles and dark mud. It was particularly in the spring months that French settlers suffered respiratory illnesses, and diseases such as cholera and pneumonia because of dampness and also poor hygiene.

The hospital in Quebec, "Hotel Dieu", run by the Crown and the Catholic Church was very quickly overwhelmed by people suffering mainly from this new illness. The doctors, healers, nuns all worked together trying to slow the spread of the disease.

Marie was enlisted by the nuns to help. For over a month she spent most of her days and sometimes nights looking after the sick, particularly the children. She found it heartbreaking to see so many young children losing their life. There were also many Amerindians affected by the pandemic and, the ones from Bidzill's tribe were so grateful when Marie could attend to them.

The hospital staff knew how important hygiene was to slow the spread of this new disease and all patients were bathed in a disinfecting lotion, including their hair, before being admitted in a clean bed. Many patients had similar symptoms: a high fever, feeling sick, diarrhoea and headaches. Some had their chest and body covered in a rash of dark spots. Though it was a new disease in Quebec, the doctors suspected, as many other contagious diseases, it was spread either by fleas or lice or both. Hygiene was very poor in Quebec's households and fleas and lice were a common occurrence.

Marie learned a lot talking to the doctors and the nuns during the epidemic. The doctors gave her advice: "Wash your hands as often as possible and put a scarf to cover your hair when looking after the patients in the hospital." She was lucky as she did not catch it. There was no cure for this but they tried to keep the patients as comfortable as possible, cooling them down to reduce their temperature and soothing their rash with a lotion. The hospital nuns also made sure that the patients drank enough to rehydrate themselves after a fever or diarrhoea.

Marie was exhausted but really happy that she could help. Some of the patients started to recover after two weeks in hospital but at least more than forty per cent of them had died. It was the worst epidemic the French settlers had experienced. Because of its cold climate and low population, until then Quebec had not experienced such a devastating disease until now.

Both Catherine's eldest boys, Philippe and Baptiste, had been struck by the disease but they recovered thanks to Marie's good advice to keep them isolated in one room with plenty of rest and drinking regularly. The rest of the family had been spared.

Among Bidzill's community there were very few casualties except for three elders who had refused to go to the hospital.

9

A NEW SPRING

A year had passed and everyone one in Quebec was looking forward to the summer months.

Joseph and Antoinette were flourishing living in the Amerindian community. Bidzill and Marie looked after them really well, as if they were their own. Both children were now speaking French and the Huron dialect fluently. Every Sunday they went to Notre Dame Church as a family. The children loved the sounds of the church bell before and after the service. There was an organist playing every Sunday and a lot of hymn singing. Joseph and Antoinette were so well behaved in the church, enchanted by the sound of music. Joseph could sometimes sing along as well, as twice a week he went to the Jesuits school where he was taught, among other things, to sing.

During the warmer months many Huron ladies also joined the Catholic celebrations and processions as they loved violin music from the Ursuline convent, as well as drums and military fife music.

The many ceremonies organised by the clergy included songs, music and hymns for every station on a procession route.

Bidzill and Marie were busy people but they always made sure that on Sundays and in the evenings to devote time to the children, talking to them and playing.

The children seem very content, thought Marie, *in spite of having lost their mother and father.* She spoke to them a lot about Marguerite: "Your mother was a clever lady, she made beautiful clothes, everyone loved her and she loved you very much." Every time they heard it the children smiled with pride at Marie.

Marie had become a very confident young woman. She had learned so much in the last year, particularly on the subject of medicine. The doctors and nuns were so impressed with her. She now spent two days a week working at the hospital helping the doctors and the other two days teaching. She was also allowed to access the hospital library to continue to improve her knowledge.

She had also been given permission to watch surgical operations performed by the surgeons. She felt very privileged; she knew women could not be doctors or surgeons but perhaps it would happen one day.

She felt very fulfilled with her life in La Nouvelle-France, she could never have dreamt of a better life. She loved her job and her husband. The only sadness was the fact Marguerite was not here anymore to share her achievement and happiness.

July had arrived and the weather was wonderfully warm. Bidzill went tracking, hunting and fishing a lot, leading the young men of his tribe. He never went away more than a few days at a time as he did not like to leave Marie and the children for too long. He had become a strong and self-assured leader, well liked and respected. His father was very proud of him. As he was coming back from one of his fishing trips at the end of July, he saw Marie coming towards him beaming. "I have some good news for you," she said smiling. "How would you like to be a papa soon?"

Bidzill rushed to embrace her and put his hands on her belly. "Really, are you sure? It's wonderful, Elu, I am going to be a dad!" He rushed to his parents' hut to tell them the news and in no time all of the Indian village knew and was congratulating both of them.

Marie confided to the nuns and doctor friends that she thought she was expecting a baby. According to them after checking her, the doctors believed she was about three months' pregnant and the baby was due sometime in February. She had wanted to be sure before telling Bidzill and the rest of the community. She felt she was ready now to have a family and Bidzill had been so patient by not trying to put pressure on her. He knew how important her work was to her and taking care of her sister's children had been a priority for her until now. She was lucky to have such an understanding husband because there was a lot of pressure from the Church and the king for married women to have children to grow the French community in Quebec.

Catherine and Pierre were very happy together. Little Marguerite was fourteen months' old now and everyone fussed around her. She was a lovely child: nice-natured with lovely red hair like her mum. The boys and Pierre spoiled her rotten and called her little princess, she was the household little sunshine. Pierre felt very fulfilled and content, he got on really well with the boys and went fishing and tracking regularly with Philippe and Baptiste.

In September he decided to go for three days to Montreal to trade the furs he had collected after tracking and hunting. He was travelling on his own using his boat. He knew a place in Montreal where he would get a good price for his furs and he could also trade them for some valuable goods.

For his two nights in Montreal, Pierre stayed in a small inn near the river. It was very basic but clean and the food was decent.

Pierre had a good first day in Montreal; he had sold or traded most of his furs and acquired some really useful goods to bring back. He had also bought some lovely cloth for Catherine and Marie so they could make new dresses.

After dinner he decided to celebrate and went to one of the lively taverns nearby. He thought he deserved a few "*eau de vie*" to chill out and was looking forward to chatting to some of the men there. He knew there would be soldiers, hunters and fishermen to chat to. Some of them would just be arriving fresh from France and he could get all the news from his homeland. The tavern was very busy; he ordered a drink and it was not long before he started chatting to a couple of soldiers. They told him how the King Louis XIV was spending more and more money on Versailles, giving outlandish soirées, whereas farmers and the rest of the population were still struggling to feed their children. The king wanted to raise taxes as his spending was out of control and he was losing popularity. The soldiers and Pierre continued to drink and chat and had a game of billiard together.

"I lost, let me buy you another drink, lads!" said Pierre. He was really enjoying the evening and the men's company.

He loved his family life but it's nice to have a break with the lads and news from his homeland, he thought. In the tavern a lot of drunken men were singing when suddenly a fight broke out. Everyone stopped to see what was happening. At the back of the inn two drunk men were hitting each other swearing and insulting each other.

Insults were flying around. "*Fripon, voleur, gueux!*" It seems one of them had stolen money from the other.

The fight was like a show for the men; they were cheering and nobody tried to stop it. At one point the tavern owner finally intervened, throwing the two men fighting out of the inn. As they were passing the crowd on their way out, Pierre could not believe it, one of the men was Antoine. "Antoine!" screamed Pierre.

Pierre rushed out to catch up with him. "Antoine, stop!" he shouted. Antoine saw him and tried to run away from him. In no time Pierre caught up with him they looked at each other as Pierre grabbed him by the neck, red with anger. They both sobered up pretty quickly with the shock of seeing each other.

"Why did you abandoned your family, you bastard, you are the lowest of the low," he screamed at Antoine. "You killed her, she loved you so much and now, there are two orphans without a mother or father, you're scum," he continued, punching Antoine as hard as he could.

Antoine tried to avoid the blows and said, "Leave me alone, loser!"

By then Pierre was hitting him so hard that Antoine fell on the ground bleeding heavily and unconscious. Other men intervened before Pierre could kill him.

"What is wrong with you?" asked one of the men. "You almost killed him!".

"He deserves it," answered Pierre adding, "this *gueux* abandoned his wife and kids and the poor woman died with a broken heart."

"I know Antoine," said one of the lads, "his wife and kid are fine living happily in Nantes."

"What did you just say?" replied Pierre. "This charlatan remarried in France while leaving his family in Quebec!" said Pierre outraged. "I am going to denounce him and expose him for his shameful behaviour!"

For Pierre to see Antoine again brought back all these awful memories. It took him a long time to recover from the death of Marguerite; losing her left a big hole in his heart as he cared so much for her. He was not sure how he was going to punish Antoine. He had been given the address of an inn where Antoine stayed when he was in Montreal but Antoine was cunning and after his encounter with Pierre, he probably would be leaving the next morning to go back to France.

The next morning Pierre rushed to the harbour trying to find Antoine. He had sobered up and he wanted to speak to him to tell him how Marguerite died and asked him if he was going to take responsibility for his two children left behind. They deserved that much after losing their mother and the fact that Joseph still remembered his father and mentioned him from time to time.

After giving it some thought, Pierre believed Antoine would feel so remorseful that he would go and see his children and even take them back to France with him. He had been good with them when he was with Marguerite and seemed to love them very much.

Antoine sadly was nowhere to be seen. Pierre felt defeated. *What should I do?*

On one hand he felt the children should be taken care of by their own father, on the other hand they were happy now with Marie and Bidzill.

Would it be too much of an upheaval for them to be uprooted to France? Besides, Antoine had not been a reliable parent so far, just a bigamist leaving behind a family to start another one!

Would his new wife accept the arrival of two children of a previous marriage? he thought.

Pierre had mixed feelings about it. Antoine had been a good friend, helpful and reliable when they went tracking and hunting in the past. They had many good times together before his departure to France.

Pierre could still not make sense of how callous Antoine had been leaving Marguerite and the children alone and worse of all starting a new life with someone else! He wished that Antoine could at least have given him some explanations but he was so drunk nothing would have made sense.

He did not think either that denouncing Antoine was the right thing to do now. Now Antoine had a new family in Bretagne, they would be the one to suffer most. Pierre wanted to speak to Antoine to shame him and make him feel guilty for his actions, he wanted to know if he felt any remorse or pain for what he had done. He wanted to tell him how beautiful and bright Joseph and Antoinette were, how he himself was married to Catherine, how happy they were and the fact they also had a lovely daughter called Marguerite.

How could their friendship have disintegrated so quickly for him to never come back?

Pierre suddenly felt such sadness, he knew he probably would never see Antoine again. His anger had vanished. *There is no point*, he thought, *to look back*. Joseph and Antoinette were happy and well looked after now. After all, it was Pierre's loss if he never saw his wonderful children again. Pierre just felt deep sorrow thinking about Marguerite and how she died losing her will to live.

The weather in Montreal was matching Pierre's sombre mood.

It was overcast, inclement and high winds started blowing the multicolour autumn leaves from the trees.

The waves of the river St. Lawrence were rocking widely from side to side and had acquired a slate-grey tone.

Pierre decided to finish his trading and go home. He could not wait to see Catherine and the children again. He was such a lucky man. The thought of it all changed his mood and he smiled to himself, looking forward to holding his baby daughter Marguerite in his arms.

He also decided he would not tell anyone about meeting Antoine except Catherine as he trusted her wisdom and he liked to share everything with her. What was the point of upsetting everyone if obviously Antoine had never had any intention of coming back.

Antoine in France

When Antoine left to go back to France, he was relieved to begin with. He felt he needed more excitement in his life for a while; Quebec was so boring during the harsh winters. He felt a bit guilty about leaving Marguerite and the children but had every intention of coming back in the spring.

When he arrived back in Nantes, he decided to call on his mother in Normandy. Last time he saw his mother she was working in a small fishing village called St. Aubin as a maid for a rich merchant family. He went back and enquired about her.

"I am afraid your mother passed away one year ago," the butler told him. "She is buried in the local cemetery, the gentleman and the lady of the house paid for the funerals as they were very fond of her, she was a good and faithful maid."

Antoine was very saddened by the news; he wanted to tell her what a good life he had in Quebec with his wife and two beautiful children. He went on her grave and said a little prayer "Rest in peace, Maman."

He decided to leave for Paris and sell the pelts and furs as he had planned. His friend Charles lived there in a small basement room in the Pigalle area and last time they met in Quebec Charles had invited him to stay with him if he ever visited. Antoine was looking forward to going, he missed the hustle and bustle of the big city. He used to love being in Paris. For him it was the centre of the world. When he arrived at his friend's place he was shattered. It took him three days to travel, getting rides from various carriages and he had not been able to get much sleep. He wanted to make sure no one could steal his precious furs. There were a lot of poor and starving people on his journey, always on the look out for an opportunity to grab whatever they could sell or trade for food.

Charles said to his friend, "Get some sleep and we'll catch up tomorrow." The room was very poorly furnished with just a small wooden table and a couple of stools. No proper beds, just a couple of dirty rugs on the floor. Antoine laid down on one of the rugs and fell asleep almost immediately. Charles was a night owl enjoying Paris night life and he disappeared to the nearest tavern across the road.

Antoine woke up early morning while Charles, not long in, was fast asleep next to him snoring loudly. After grabbing a piece of bread and drinking some water from the jar on the table, Antoine left to go and see the merchants he knew of. They were knowledgeable about quality furs and pelts and they had a good base of rich clients ready to pay well for good-quality furs.

He only took four with him to show the merchants, the rest was left in the heavy trunk at Charles's.

The merchants were impressed and three of them promised a good and fair price, particularly for beaver pelts. The pelts were in great demand as it was used mainly to make felt hats which were very popular and fashionable. Beaver stuffing was ideal for yarning and therefore required in quantity by hat makers.

One of the rich merchants, Monsieur Perrin, had been very impressed by Antoine and told him: "Come back with all your fur stocks, I promise to pay you top price for them as they are really good quality."

Antoine was very pleased to sell all his furs to him as it was saving him from going around for new buyers.

Monsieur Perrin kept his word and Antoine could hardly believe the amount of money he made. He thought, *I'll show Pierre when I get back that this trip was well worth it*! Monsieur Perrin wanted Antoine to stay in touch with him and invited him for dinner the following week. He thought Antoine could become a regular fur provider for his shop.

Antoine was flattered by the invitation and the trust Monsieur Perrin had in him. Meantime, he enjoyed his time in Paris with his friend Charles. They went across the road to the tavern every night. In the tavern there was a lot of gambling going on over card games. To start with Antoine was careful but after a few drinks, encouraged by

Charles, his good earnings were disappearing fast. Every night he thought he could win back what he had lost.

The night he was invited for dinner he stayed sober to make a good impression and keep in Monsieur Perrin's good books. The evening went very well. Madame Perrin was a kind and friendly woman and the food was delicious. What really took Charles by surprise was to meet their daughter Victorine. She was beautiful, lively and very amusing. Antoine was smitten as soon as he met her. He thought, *no, I am a married man with children, I must not think about her.*

He had not told Monsieur Perrin he was married with children and as he never wore his wedding ring the question never arose.

Monsieur Perrin thought Antoine had a good eye for quality furs and asked if he would be interested in working for him as his main supplier. "You don't necessarily need to go and do the tracking and hunting but just buy for me the best quality ones when you go back to Quebec. You would be the go-between and I will pay you well."

Antoine told him he would think about it and get back to him.

When he told Charles about the offer his friend told him he would be a fool not to accept. "You have hardly any money left after your gambling losses, before going back to your family you need to earn it back."

Antoine felt ashamed. It was true, he had lost most of the good earnings he made with selling his stock of furs. A week later he went back to speak to Monsieur Perrin and told him he accepted his offer. He would not be able to go back to Quebec before the spring but Charles was happy to have him around. As he was leaving Monsieur Perrin's shop, Victorine ran after him and shouted, "Monsieur Lemarin, would you care to accompany me to the park. I need a chaperone."

"With pleasure," he replied, flattered.

It was the beginning of a great romance. They met every day for a walk in the park and Antoine started to be invited regularly for dinner at the Perrins'. It was now February and still unaware Antoine was already married, Monsieur Perrin suggested one day. "Why don't you two get married, you are made for each other and we are so fond of you, Antoine."

Antoine was so smitten with Victorine and feeling so welcomed by her wealthy family that he had put Marguerite and the children at the back of his mind and hardly spared them a thought. Looking back at his past life, in a flash he knew already what his answer was going to be.

The only regret he felt was the fact he would never again see his children. He particularly loved his firstborn son Joseph very much. In contrast, he hardly knew his daughter Antoinette as she was just a baby when he left. He finally made up his mind, quickly thinking he had been so tired of Marguerite low moods after giving birth, she was not the fun girl he had met and fallen in love with.

On impulse he answered, "Yes, of course. I love your daughter," smiling at Victorine.

He spoke to Charles later, "What have I done! But I am happy here and I love Victorine, her father is a rich man and after all, life is made for living, no one will ever know! Please, Charles, promise me you won't tell a soul about this".

"Fine, I promised but it does not mean I approve." He sighed.

Charles made a living mainly from gambling. He had no strong moral values but having been abandoned by his father himself, he felt quite critical of Antoine's deceit.

The marriage was a grand affair and many well-to-do families were invited. Antoine had mentioned he had no family left as his mother had passed away three years ago in Normandy.

After the wedding Monsieur Perrin decided the couple should go and live in Brittany where he owned a big property. He believed it would make it easier for Antoine to travel back and forth to Montreal. He expected Antoine to make regular trips to Paris as well to bring back the merchandise. Victorine was happy with the arrangement as Brittany was the holiday home in her childhood, she had friends there and Nantes was a pleasant town. After settling in the town of Nantes, the couple was very happy. Monsieur Perrin had provided the couple with a substantial rent which allowed them to enjoy a very comfortable life.

In late summer Antoine needed to go to Montreal to purchase furs for Monsieur Perrin. When he arrived in Montreal he settled in a small inn near the harbour. He planned to stay around three to four weeks and catch the last boat back to France before the big frost.

He had no intention, of course, to go back to Marguerite

and the children, his life in France was so comfortable. He had a nice big house and was a fairly wealthy man.

He really was hoping he would not meet any of his old acquaintances. *Most of them are around the town of Quebec,* he thought, *so I should be quite safe.* The first three weeks Antoine managed to acquire a large stock of good-quality fur: mainly beaver pelts and some foxes. He was very pleased with himself. He had been able to barter and get them at the best price. In the evenings he would get back to the tavern and after his dinner go around all the other port taverns and get drunk, sometimes he would meet some of the men he knew in Nantes and who made the journey with him to Montreal. He loved the freedom and the buzz of drinking spirits. It made him feel invincible and he would often pick a fight with a fellow drinker just for the fun of it. It reminded it of the good old days when he was young and free to do whatever he wanted.

He surprised himself by not thinking much about his previous life in Quebec. Victorine and France was his life now. He went back to France at the beginning of October, bringing back a really good cargo of furs. Monsieur Perrin was delighted with Antoine's purchases and told him, "I knew I could count on you."

Victorine was now expecting a baby for the spring and her family was overjoyed. Spring arrived and Victorine gave birth to a healthy girl. They called her Helene. The christening took place in Nantes and many friends and relatives took part in the ceremony. Antoine enjoyed his notoriety. He was well known and respected in Nantes. It was a small town and until now his past has not caught up with him.

It was two years later during one of his stays in Montreal that one night he had an unlucky encounter with Pierre. They fought and Antoine beat him up quite badly, he also remembered in his drunken state some of the things Pierre shouted at him about Marguerite and the children. He decided it was best to hide and leave as soon as possible. He did not feel any remorse. he just wanted to get back to his good life in France. He was only hoping no one would find out in Nantes or Paris.

Back in France he worried for a few months but very soon life was back to normal, with no threats coming his way.

10

WINTER CHALLENGES AND A SURPRISE

It was a bitter, cold winter again. The snow was piling up and it was difficult to travel with the storms and snow drifts.

Marie was heavily pregnant now and everyone was telling her to rest and take it easy, she was also extremely big for her small frame. The Indian ladies were saying it is going to be a very big and tall baby, not an easy delivery. Because of the bad weather Marie had not been able to go to the convent or the hospital to help since the New year. However, she was glad as she felt exhausted.

Bidzill was very attentive and a bit worried about Marie's size and tiredness. He wanted Marie to be checked by the doctors at the hospital to make sure everything was well but travelling just now was too treacherous. He would try to take her there as soon as the stormy weather stopped. It was the beginning of February and the baby was due approximately at the end of the month. All the

Indian medicine ladies were watching Marie, making sure she put her feet up and gave her some medicinal drinks to relieve her heartburn and indigestion. Marie felt so grateful to have such good care and attention. Joseph kept coming to see her, smiling and saying, "*Le bebe de Marie,*" putting his little hand on Marie's tummy.

She smiled and answered, "Soon you will have a baby cousin to play with."

The bad weather finally lifted and the blizzard had stopped. As the snow was four feet high it was impossible for Bidzill to use a carriage to take Marie to hospital. He really wanted her to be checked, as she looked to be in pain and was always so tired. He decided to use an Indian sledge to take Marie to hospital. It would be a hazardous journey in the snow but his trusted friend Hawk decided to accompany them and help with the sledging.

It took a few hours to reach Quebec's Hotel-Dieu and it was almost four in the afternoon and dark already when they arrived. They helped Marie to get inside the building. There were a lot of familiar faces greeting them, so pleased to see Marie. Doctor Martinet, who knew Marie well as she helped a lot during the epidemic, told her to lay down so he could examine her and see how the baby was doing. He bent and put his ear on Marie's stomach to hear the baby's heartbeat. He spent a few minutes moving his head around with a puzzled look.

"What's wrong?" asked Bidzill, looking alarmed.

Doctor Martinet continued his examination, silently checking Marie's pulse and palming her stomach area asking if she felt any movements or pains. Marie said she had a lot of heartburns and pains when the baby was kicking.

The doctor enquired, "What side do you feel the baby is kicking?"

"It seems to be both sides really and often," replied Marie.

"Well, I think you'll need to stay with us in the hospital until the birth," said Doctor Martinet.

"Why is there a problem, is my baby alright?" cried Marie, looking at Bidzill wearily.

Doctor Martinet finally smiled and told them, "I think you are expecting twins, Marie, I am pretty sure I heard two heartbeats! We need to keep an eye on you as they are due very soon."

Both Bidzill and Marie were speechless. "Twins, my Elu, it is wonderful," said Bidzill finally leaning to Marie to kiss her, smiling now.

"Go home, Bidzill, Marie needs to rest now, you can come back tomorrow," said Doctor Martinet.

Bidzill left full of joy. He could not wait to tell his family, he felt exhausted suddenly but he was so proud. Marie was in good hands for the delivery and that reassured him.

Marie fell asleep quickly. She was so tired after her journey but she did not sleep well. She was very restless because she was carrying so much weight and was finding it difficult to find a comfortable position.

Bidzill arrived back to his village really late in the night. It was a difficult journey back to the Huron village in the snow and he struggled with his companion in the dark to manoeuvre the sledge.

The next day he rushed to his family to announce the news about the forthcoming births. His wise parents and elders told him to curb his enthusiasm until the arrival of the babies. There were quite a lot of superstitions in the community and the elders were aware that it would be a difficult birth for Marie. Babies and mothers often died in childbirth, particularly with multiple births.

Joseph and Antoinette were asking about their auntie Marie, very excited about having a little cousin. Bidzill spent the morning with them but did not mention Marie was expecting twins. He just said let's wait and see. He had listened to the elders and decided to be more cautious about telling others. He could not wait to see Marie again and was so worried now. He could not bear the thought of losing Marie. It would be terrible to lose the babies but losing Marie was unthinkable for him, he loved her so much.

The weather had deteriorated again and Bidzill had to wait another day before being able to go back to the hospital. Many of the Indian tribes were having rituals, wishing for Marie to have a good birth.

Meanwhile, there were a lot of activities in the Indian village.

The men were getting ready for war as the different Iroquois tribes were fighting among themselves. An imminent battle was brewing with a neighbouring village nearby.

Wonderful news

When Bidzill made it to the hospital the next day he was desperate to see Marie. It was late morning and he ran to the ward where she was. He could see Marie fast asleep and panicked thinking she was very poorly. The doctor arrived and when he saw Bidzill's distraught look, very quickly said to him, "Don't worry, Marie is very tired, she was in labour for ten hours and she lost a lot of blood but she is fine now."

Bidzill looked around, still worried, and asked: "And the babies?"

"They are fine. You are the proud father of a little boy who was the first born, his sister was born twenty minutes later," said the doctor.

It took a while for Bidzill to compose himself and finally smiling, answered, "I am a dad now and they are all fine?"

He did not know whether to laugh or cry, so happy but in shock.

One of the nuns called him and said: "Let Marie rest, she needs it and come and see your babies!"

The babies were still receiving special care as they were tiny but hopefully Marie would be able to breastfeed them and they would be able to go home soon.

Bidzill was so proud as he held the tiny babies in his arm.

"Do you have a name for them?" asked the nun. "They will need to be christened as soon as possible, it is important," she added, never forgetting her holy duty.

Marie and Bidzill had already chosen Christian names for their babies before the birth for either a boy or a girl, just in case the babies didn't survive the birth as it often was the case for multiple births.

Bidzill said, smiling, "Anne and Louis." They were their two favourite names. They had agreed on Louis in honour of the French King Louis the XIV. Without his policy of sending young ladies to Quebec, Marie and Bidzill would never have met. Anne was a good name short and easy to pronounce, they thought. They had planned to also have an Indian name for the children so they could celebrate their Indian roots as well but Bidzill did not mentioned it to the nun.

It was five days after the birth that Bidzill could finally come home with Marie and the two babies. Louis and Anne were feeding well and had put some weight on. Though Anne was the bigger baby, both were doing well.

Marie was still nervous about being a new mother with two newborns. Bidzill reassured her, "I'll help you, my Elu, and all the ladies in my tribe cannot wait to see the children and help too. Everyone is so proud of you." She had been well cared for at the hospital and felt very secure there. She was happy, however, to go back home and show off her babies, just a bit anxious.

When Bidzill, Marie and the twins arrived back at the Indian village they could not have imagined a better homecoming. It was a real feast, a great quantity of food had been prepared, and all the community was patiently queuing to see the babies and congratulate the new parents. First the elders came, followed by adults and finally the children. The children were so well behaved as they were told to be quiet so not to upset the newborns. Joseph and Antoinette came too, they were really happy to see the babies and Marie back home. They had missed her a lot as for them she was like their mother. Joseph still remembered Marguerite and sometimes mentioned her but for little Antoinette the memory of her mother had faded away, she was so young when she lost her.

The following day Catherine and Pierre came to visit with their boys and young Marguerite. They marvelled to see the two tiny babies sleeping so peacefully.

11

FIVE YEARS LATER

Life had been good for Marie and Bidzill. The twins were now five years old and thriving. They were also bilingual and spent a lot of time playing with their cousins Joseph and Antoinette who kept a protective eye on them.

Two more siblings had been born since. Two boys: Leon, aged three and Francois, aged one. Marie breastfed all her babies for the first three months but each time she ran out of milk. She was lucky as some of the Huron ladies in the community who had babies took the task of breastfeeding Marie's babies. It was the custom for the Hurons to breastfeed children until they were two or three years old and Marie was happy and grateful that the Indian community took good care of the children.

She had been consequently able to continue teaching orphans at the convent as well as helping at the hospital from time to time. She had gained a lot of respect from the doctors and nuns for her knowledge. She had learned so much also from the Indian shamans to cure some local illnesses that the French medical community never hesitated for asking her opinion and help.

Marie tried, however, to spend more time with her own children and as she was expecting another child, she had the idea that eventually she would start a school in the Indian village; it would give her the opportunity to spend more time with her own children and the Huron. The idea also appealed to the Jesuits because she would be a strong asset to them teaching French to the indigenous community as well as teaching them Christian values and faith.

Bidzill and Marie had also remained close friends with Pierre and Catherine and little Marguerite had turned into a beautiful and clever seven years old. Still really spoiled by the boys and her father but she was a kind little girl in spite of being headstrong and opinionated. Marie thought it was a good thing as one day, like her, Marguerite would confidently stand on her own two feet and be strong. Marie could not help thinking about her sister and how sadly her life had turned out.

The two sisters had such big dreams when they arrived in Quebec. For Marie the life of her dream had surpassed her expectations. She was very happily married with a good man and fulfilled as a mother, at the same time she was able to pursue her career and enjoyed the learning and challenges she was experiencing every day.

Marguerite, on the other hand, had been let down so badly. For Marie, thinking about Marguerite was the only time she felt sad because her sister was not here anymore to share her success and happiness. Marguerite would never see her own children and Marie's children grow up. She felt comforted though when she saw Marguerite's children so happy and confident. One day she would tell them about their story and how the two sisters from an orphanage arrived in La Nouvelle-France to start a new and better life.

Joseph was very fond of Bidzill and always looked up to him. Bidzill had become a father figure for him and they had developed a close bond. Bidzill took Joseph fishing from time to time and they both enjoyed each other's company. Joseph was a funny young boy full of joy and energy.

Catherine and Pierre were also very happy. Regularly Pierre would go to Marguerite's grave and deposit a bunch of wildflowers. It was a memory of the past. He was not sad anymore about Marguerite's fate, *it is just life,* he thought. He was so grateful now for his good life in Quebec, his happiness and especially his wonderful family.

12

A NEW GENERATION

Philippe was now a young man and he had announced one day that he had decided to join the priesthood. The Jesuits were really happy to have him as he was such a bright young man. Pierre and Catherine were not surprised as he had always been very religious, praying and going to church regularly. They were in fact very proud of him. It had really been his choice with no pressure from them. It was usually common for French families to want their firstborn to go into priesthood or for the eldest daughter to become a nun.

Baptiste, on the other hand, preferred farming and hunting and in the summer went hunting and tracking for 3 months with two other friends. He was happy and still enjoyed working at the farm the rest of the time.

He also seemed to be courting a young lady called Paulette that he had met outside the church one Sunday after Mass. Paulette was the daughter of a local farmer and Baptiste had been very impressed with her farming skills.

She was able to deal with all kind of tasks whether it was indoors with cooking and sewing or outdoors looking after the farm animals or the land. Paulette thought that Baptiste was so handsome and quite a catch coming from such a good family. They were in love and it would not be long before they decided to marry. Catherine and Pierre really liked Paulette, they thought she was a sensible and down-to-earth girl and would make a good wife for Baptiste.

Pierre was now a very successful farmer, trader and builder; he had bought more land and employed more workers to help him with farming. He also had started building more houses for new comers with Baptiste's help. It was a very lucrative business because with new settlers and an increase population the demand was high. Catherine also employed a young indigenous girl to help her with the house chores. Both were good employers, they treated workers well with a fair wage, which was not always the case in Quebec.

Young Marguerite was now ten years old. She was her father's darling and knew how to get around his little finger. She was still a delightful young girl, hot-headed but full of fun and kind to everybody. After Marguerite, Catherine and Pierre had tried to have more children but unfortunately they failed and therefore they concentrated on growing their farm and business. They were nevertheless very happy with their life. Pierre and Catherine had become pillars of the community in Quebec and many new settlers visited them to ask for advice. Both were always kind and helpful, sometimes helping the poorest settlers financially.

The boys and young Marguerite were all doing well. Marguerite had private tutoring, she was bright and could read and write fluently now as well as being good with numbers.

She kept teasing her two teenage brothers, Robert and Paul: "I'll be running the farm when I grow up."

They smiled and answered back, "We'll see about that." The two farm hands who originally stayed with Marguerite had died four years previously. The whole family was devastated when Jacques suddenly collapsed in the field while he was picking beans; his heart had failed him. His friend Francois died a few weeks later in his bed; no one knew the cause but both men were quite elderly and they had worked hard all their life. Catherine and Pierre had advised them many times to take it easy and rest as they already had plenty of workers but they enjoyed working and helping, that's the only life they knew. Pierre and Catherine had informed their family but none of their relatives were present at the funerals, probably because they lived so far away and the trip would have been too long.

Joseph had grown to be a strong boy at fourteen and kept following Bidzill everywhere, helping him with his tasks. He was part of the tribe now and could hunt and fish.

Bidzill was now the chief of his community; both his parents had passed away. He was well liked for his fairness and leadership and Joseph wanted to follow in his footsteps. Being brought up by the indigenous community, Joseph felt more Huron than French now. He admired them and felt one of them.

He sometimes asked Bidzill and Marie: "What happened to my parents?"

It was a difficult question to answer and Marie would say: "Your mum was unwell and she collapsed in the cold and your father, we are not sure if he perished when he went back to France to sell his furs." They added that they hadn't heard from him since he left.

Both Marie and Bidzill felt it was not necessary to tell the truth as it would be too painful for him. They also worried that Joseph might want to go to France to find his father as they both believed Antoine had abandoned his family, though Pierre never mentioned his encounter with Antoine in Montreal.

Marie, on the other hand, often kept talking to Antoinette and Joseph about their mother. "She was a wonderful sister and mother," she told them. "She was very pretty and clever and when you two were born she always said it was the best day of her life, she loved you very much."

Marie also told them about their childhood in the orphanage and how good Marguerite had been with her. She told them how lucky they were to have such a good life in Quebec and it was all due to Marguerite's initiative. Joseph and Antoinette felt very proud of their mother after hearing Marie. It was important and comforting to remind them they had a loving mother.

Antoinette was a caring girl, doting on her younger cousins but nowadays she always seemed a bit sad. Marie worried about her as she looked so much like her beloved sister.

Unlike her brother Joseph she did not seem to fit in either with the Hurons or with her French community. She was, however, very religious and prayed a lot and the nuns at the convent saw her as a potential recruit to their order.

Marie felt Antoinette, aged thirteen, was too young to make a decision and told the nuns she preferred to wait and see. Antoinette was very close to her brother Joseph and seemed to worship him. She would wait anxiously for his return after each of his outings with Bidzill. She had become a reserved and introverted teenage girl and Joseph seemed to be the only person she talked to and confided in.

Joseph was flattered and quite protective of her and this appeared enough for Antoinette. Marie tried to get closer to her niece, speaking to her and spending time alone with her but Antoinette, as she was growing up, remained reserved and guarded. Her attitude made Marie sad as she had been so close to her sister and she wanted so strongly for Antoinette to be happy. She just decided to keep an eye on her and keep her safe, that's all she could do at the moment. Marie's only comfort regarding Antoinette was to see how happy she was looking after young children. It was the only time she saw her smile and laugh as she seemed to have such a strong maternal instinct and it was reassuring to see how the children loved her too. The twins Louis and Anne were particularly fond of Antoinette and she showed them endless patience and kindness playing and looking after them.

Marie was hoping Antoinette was just going through a difficult teenage stage and that hopefully her moody phase would improve with time.

There was another worry for Marie as tension was rising between the Hurons, who were allied to other local tribes, and the Iroquois, their sworn enemy. There had been a few battles already between the tribes and each time she feared for Bidzill life as he was leading his men.

The Hurons usually were backing the French settlers, whereas the Iroquois were backing the English settlers further south. An impending serious big fight was brewing between the tribes and Marie knew that Bidzill and his men would be taking part.

The Iroquois had grown bolder and often were attacking, isolating French farms and towns spreading fear throughout New France. The King of France had sent more troups and soldiers to build several new fortifications in Fort Richelieu and alongside the St. Lawrence and Richelieu rivers. Those were the strategic areas for both parties for communication and navigation.

While the French soldiers were busy protecting the area, Bidzill, with his men and his allied, were getting ready for another battle against the Iroquois south of Quebec. Marie could not hide her worry as she feared for Bidzill and his men.

She hated war and the destruction and death which followed. There was nothing she could do to stop him. He was the chief and his pride and honour commanded him to go, it was his duty and role to lead and protect others.

It was spring but the ground was still very muddy with melting snow the day Bidzill and his men left for battle armed with all the weapons at their disposal: spears, lances, pikes, swords, hatchets and halberds.

What added to Marie's distress was the fact that Joseph, just short of his fifteenth birthday, had insisted to go along and nothing could persuade him not to go. "I am a fit young man now and I can prove it, Bidzill needs my help," he said defiantly.

His sister Antoinette had also begged him not to go but he dismissed all her objections and did not give in to her tears.

The battle was very bloody; many men on both sides were left dead or injured in mucky and slushy fields. Bidzill's men had won the battle but at a cost. Bidzill was alive and counting the men he had lost, amounting to ten, and twenty were injured. He was desperately looking for Joseph, who had been hit by a spear. He had seen him falling earlier but was unable to intervene at the time as he was fighting. Bidzill walked up and down the battlefield calling Joseph.

One of his men shouted, "Found him, here."

Bidzill rushed to find Joseph lying unconscious but alive.

He seemed to have a superficial head wound but blood was gushing out of his right leg and a bone was sticking out. It was a nasty injury. Would he survive? Could he bring him back quickly enough to the hospital to be examined by a doctor? He asked one of his valid men to take charge and see to the other wounded men.

He picked up Joseph and carried him until he could

find help. He kept talking to Joseph saying, "Stay with me, son, stay with me."

He finally reached a monastery where one of the priests managed to stop the bleeding on Joseph's leg.

"Take him to the Hotel Dieu Hospital as quickly as possible or he won't survive. It is a bad injury, he's lost a lot of blood," he told Bidzill.

The monastery put a carriage at their disposal and Joseph was rushed to "L'Hotel Dieu". It was the best hospital in Quebec to give Joseph a chance to survive his injury.

Some of the doctors recognised Marie's husband and rushed to help Joseph. "His head injury is not too bad, it is mainly concussion but his leg is so bad I am not sure if we can save his leg or him," said one of the doctors.

"Please do your best to save him," murmured Bidzill, distraught at the sight of the injury.

He sat down waiting while the doctors attended to Joseph. He was exhausted after the battle and shocked by what happened to Joseph. He felt that he had not protected him from the harshness of war. He should never have accepted to take him to the battle; he was so young. Bidzill felt so guilty. What was he going to say to Marie and Antoinette? They will never forgive him if Joseph dies.

Bidzill waited all night, hardly able to get any sleep. It was midday when a nursing nun brought him a piece of bread and a bowl of soup.

"Your friend is asleep now. The surgeon repaired his leg as much as it was possible but it is too early to say whether he will survive," she told him.

"His leg was in a really bad shape and if he survives, he'll never be able to walk normally as many nerves and tendons were damaged and left him paralysed," she added.

Bidzill was devastated. "How long will he have to stay in hospital if he survives?" he asked.

"I am not sure, probably a few weeks," said the nun.

Bidzill did not know what to do. He wanted to stay and find out if Joseph would make it. On the other hand, he felt it was his duty to go back to the village and tell them what happened. The battle had been won but at what cost. Many of the families in his community had lost a member and he had to speak to all of them. He was dreading, however, telling Marie and Antoinette about Joseph.

At least Joseph was still alive at the moment, which was of some comfort to Bidzill. He started to pray, "Please, God, let him live, I beg you," and recited a paternoster. For the first time in his life Bidzill felt in need of faith, his conversion to Catholicism helped him and gave him the strength to carry on and cope.

He suddenly stood up to go home and told the nun, "I'll be back soon, take good care of him."

"We'll all pray for him" she murmured as he left.

It was late evening and already dark when Bidzill reached his village. His men had not returned yet from the battlefield, probably as they were delayed by helping the wounded, either taking them to get seen to at the hospital or coming back at a slow pace with the ones less severely injured.

When Marie saw Bidzill she rushed to meet him and take him in her arms. She was so relieved to see him then she turned round and asked, "Where are your men, where is Joseph? You look exhausted, what happened?"

Bidzill sighed and in a low voice told Marie, "We won the battle but I lost quite a few good men, I'll have to speak to their families at sunrise."

He hesitated, not sure how to tell Marie about Joseph. "Joseph is wounded and he is in hospital," he finally said with such a defeated look and tone.

Marie asked warily, "Is it serious? Is he going to survive?"

She knew Bidzill so well she could see the distress and sadness in his eyes. She kept a steady and calm voice to not add to the trauma that Bidzill had been through. She was very aware that fighting and losing some of his men had been very difficult for him so she asked again gently: "What happened to Joseph?"

"He had a head wound and a very serious injury to his leg, the head wound is not serious but his leg is very damaged. He also lost so much blood doctors are not sure whether he will survive."

Marie's eyes filled with tears she could not help herself. "What are we going to tell Antoinette?" She was thinking aloud now.

She could see Bidzill was completely shattered. "Let's go to bed now, you must rest. We can decide tomorrow what to do. I am so glad you are alive. I love you," she added quietly.

The next day all his men who survived were back at the village exhausted but relieved to have made it back. Bidzill held a council for all the fighter's families. He told them how bravely all the men fought and that they had won the battle. He also expressed his sorrow for the men who had lost their life and reassured them that the community would make sure to support the wives and children left behind. He continued, telling them, "We will organise a big ceremony to honour our dead. We will have a church service for the ones who converted to Catholicism as well as a native traditional ceremony for our community." As he was speaking you could hear the women and children crying and the men bowing their head.

Marie spoke to Antoinette about Joseph first thing in the morning before Bidzill addressed the community. She listened, bewildered, and started crying, "When can I see him? I want to see him!" cried Antoinette.

"We'll go to the hospital this afternoon," Marie answered quietly, praying he would still be alive as she did not have the courage to tell Antoinette how serious Joseph's injuries were and whether he would survive.

Afternoon came, it was sunny and there was some warmth in the air as Bidzill, Marie and Antoinette started their journey to the hospital.

Both Bidzill and Marie started to warn Antoinette that her brother was very ill and there was a chance that he might not overcome his injuries.

Bidzill told Antoinette: "Yesterday when I left Joseph was still unconscious, the doctors mended his leg but he lost a lot of blood before reaching the hospital."

She listened quietly and Bidzill warned her, "Even if he makes it, he will never be able to walk again, be prepared."

"I don't care if he cannot walk again, I just want him to live and I'll help him if he cannot walk properly," she answered looking at Marie and Bidzill with such a determined stare.

They finally arrived late afternoon at the "Hotel Dieu".

All were silent and anxious as they were entering the ward.

The nun who had been attending Joseph walked towards them. "He woke up but he is still very weak, you can see him but he won't be able to speak to you yet."

Antoinette was the first one to rush to her brother's bed.

She sat next to him holding his hand. "Joseph, it's me, Toinette, I am so glad you are alive, I'll help you and pray for you, don't worry."

Marie had tears in her eyes; it was so touching to hear Antoinette, still a girl at thirteen, to be so caring and loving towards her brother.

Joseph was not yet able to talk to them but at least he was still alive. They all went back home hoping that Joseph's health would improve in the next few days, *he is young and strong after all*, thought Marie.

The next few days proved very difficult for Joseph, he was now fully conscious but in terrible pain. It was not good news: the wound on his leg was infected and the surgeon finally decided to amputate Joseph's right leg below the knee.

Joseph was distraught. "What I am going to do with only one good leg, I am still young but I'll be no use to anyone," he told the doctors and his family. They all tried to reassure him. "You are lucky to be alive with this kind of injury," the doctors told him.

"We'll be here for you," Bidzill and Marie added.

The operation went well but it took a few weeks before Joseph was allowed to leave the hospital.

He struggled to walk with his crutches to begin with but after a few days he was managing quite well. Once back at the Amerindian village everyone made a fuss. Men came up to him congratulating him and telling him he was a hero for having fought so bravely.

"You deserve the name the Hurons gave you: Waya," they told him, "Because you fought like a wolf."

For the first few days Joseph felt relieved to be back home and enjoyed the attention he was given by everyone. The novelty wore off after a while and Joseph started feeling really downbeat, not knowing what he was going to do as a maimed young man.

He was feeling fed up with the help he was getting and was snapping quite a lot at his sister Antoinette. "Leave me alone, don't you have anything else to do!" he would shout at her.

"I like helping you and being with you," she pleaded.

It was too much for Joseph and he was getting meaner and meaner to her. "You're like a parasite, I can't stand it, get away from me!" Antoinette would go outside and cry her heart out not knowing what to do.

Joseph felt really low, he felt useless. What was he going to do for the rest of his life.

Bidzill and Marie realised how distressed Joseph was and after discussing it they decided they should find him a task which would help restore his confidence and give him a new purpose and opportunity. The question was what kind of tasks?

After giving it some thought, Marie said, "Well, he speaks French and the Hurons language fluently, he has also a good command of Iroquois dialect, he could be a good trader interpreter between the French and the natives."

"Yes, that's true," added Bidzill. "Now we have signed a peace treaty with the Iroquois trading will be good for all of us. If Joseph manages to ride a horse again, though he probably would have to relearn using his good leg, he will be independent and of great service to us."

Both were pleased with the idea but would they be able to convince Joseph?

When they asked, Joseph sounded a bit reluctant, he did not seem to believe in himself anymore. "Riding a horse again? I don't think so, I won't be able to," he answered with his head down.

"Why don't you give it a try? Your mother would be very proud of you if you did and so would we," added Marie with an encouraging smile.

"Fine, I'll give it a try but don't expect too much, my injured leg still hurts."

It took Joseph a few days to relearn to ride. He fell off the horse many times at first and felt sorry for himself saying: "I will never manage, I am useless, forget it, I cannot do it!"

He was such an angry and frustrated young man. What was adding to his anger was the fact that he did not like being help for getting on the horse it made him feel weak.

After many attempts by swinging the half of his maimed upper leg he was able to get on the horse by himself. It was an achievement for him and it gave him the will to continue and improve.

It was a month later when he left for his first trading mission. Everyone was so proud of his efforts. His anger and bad temper had receded and he had become much kinder to his sister again, thanking her for her help and patience.

Meanwhile, Baptiste had the idea of making a wooden stump and strapping it to Joseph upper leg so he could walk more evenly and without crutches.

Joseph was reluctant to use it to begin with but after practising he gained so much freedom using it that he was very grateful to have it. He could only use it for a few hours at a time, however, because after a while the rubbing of the strut on his scared leg was very painful even when protected by a thick, soft, cotton cloth.

Joseph had found a new role and appeared quite content but there were days when he was not busy trading that he felt down and moody. He was included in many of the men's activities such as fishing and hunting but often it was too tiring for him. He also was a young man now and very keen to meet a girl he could perhaps marry one day but who would want him. He despaired.

He had his eyes on a pretty young native called "Dyani" meaning deer in Huron dialect. She had beautiful doe-brown eyes, he thought. They looked at each other shyly a few times but never spoke. "I am sure she feels sorry for me." That was the only comment he made to Marie when she mentioned that Dyani seems to like him.

Dyani, meantime, was trying to befriend Antoinette. She wanted to get to know Joseph, she liked him too and was hoping his sister would one day introduce her to him.

During the long winter months Joseph had very little work to do and he was feeling very low. The other young men in the village would come and try to cheer him up, chatting to him and playing games but it made very little difference.

"With the snow and ice outside I cannot help any of you or do anything," he told them in a gloomy voice, "please get on with your life, don't waste your time with me!"

Antoine

Antoine was still living in Brittany with Victorine and his daughter Helene. They had not been able to have more children after Victorine lost her second baby, a boy, in childbirth. The death had been very upsetting for the family. Antoine was particularly affected as he so wanted to have a son. He often thought about his son Joseph, it was the only regret he felt about leaving Marguerite. He was missing his son.

Antoine was getting older now and his hair was silvery. He was still, however, a strong and handsome man. He was not trading furs anymore. He had made enough money and the demand had slowed down, besides Mr. Perrin had retired and his nephew was running the business.

Antoine had become a bit restless again. His marriage to Victorine had lasted but there was no more excitement in his life. He was very fond of his daughter Helene, almost eleven now, and she was a sweet girl with her father's good looks, but he could not take her fishing or hunting which were his favourite hobbies. He was bored; he needed some adventures.

Antoine spoke to some of his friends about it and a well-connected gentleman in the French army suggested he could get him a six-month post in the king's army if he was interested.

In Montreal they needed someone to be in charge of a one-hundred man garrison. The king gave orders to protect the fort of Ville-Marie. "It is yours if you want the post?" said his friend. Antoine did not hesitate. The king needed more soldiers, he will become one for six months. In spite of being an older man with no army experience it would not be too much hardship. As a sergeant major he would get good accommodation and mainly give orders and supervise the soldiers.

He was lucky to get such a high rank posting having never been a soldier before but it was all to do with his standing in Nantes and connections. Antoine benefited from the fact that the king needed to recruit more soldiers and as an older man with previous experience of La Nouvelle-France it was a welcome advantage.

Victorine was upset about his decision, however, there was very little she could do to stop him. Antoine had always been a very determined man. He told her, "It is only for six months including the sea crossing." He also said to his daughter Helene, kissing her, "With your mum, look after each other while I am gone, my darling daughter." He left Nantes in March accompanied by fifty soldiers to join the rest of the garrison.

When the ship docked in Montreal at the beginning of April, Antoine and the soldiers were looking forward to settling into their new role. It took a while for Antoine to get to know his soldiers and assert his authority among them as some of them were very experienced army hands. After a couple of months Antoine became a sergeant major. He was firm and strict with the soldiers but he was a man's man; he could relax and share a drink with them when they were off duty.

13

THE DAY OF RECKONING

Spring and summer arrived in Quebec and with them the numerous activities which would provide food and shelter during the cold winter months.

Pierre was now employing trackers, hunters and fishermen, many of them were natives and very experienced. It was again a very successful season. He would be able to go to Montreal and trade or sell the furs and the fish which would be transported back to France. The harvest of fruits and vegetables had been very good too, perhaps he could take some of it there as well.

Pierre and Baptiste were getting ready for their trip to Montreal. They were going to go down on their boat and stay for four days to conclude all their trading and sales.

They now had some regular customers and buyers. They would be getting top prices for the beaver pelts which were still very much in demand in some parts of Europe. The fish trade was also good once they were gutted, dried or smoked and packaged for travel. Each trip they stayed in the same *auberge*: "Le Cheval Blanc". They knew the owner, a man called Jacques originally from Normandy. Jacques had failed at making money hunting and tracking but he was a good cook and settled in Montreal after buying a small inn close to the harbour. He was a friendly man and had a steady clientele coming regularly to dine or spend a few nights. Pierre had stayed in Le Cheval Blanc during his previous trip to Montreal and befriended Jacques.

Before their departure they visited Bidzill and Marie. Baptiste, who was a good friend of Joseph, noticed how morose he had been lately, in spite of the good summer weather, and said to Joseph, "We are going to Montreal, why don't you come with us. It will be fun, what do you say?"

"I am not sure," replied Joseph.

"You can help us, you are good at negotiating!" Baptiste did not give Joseph a chance to refuse the offer. "Pierre, Joseph is coming with us to Montreal!" he shouted for everyone to hear.

"Great, looking forward to have you on board," said Pierre encouragingly.

It was early morning mid-August when the three men left for Montreal. Their trip on the river was uneventful apart from being pestered by mosquitoes swarming around the boat early evening. The good summer weather was great except for the millions of mosquitoes which usually came with it. When they finally arrived at their destination, they moored the boat, securing their goods and paying a local watchman for the night. They headed for Le Cheval

Blanc inn, happy to get a good night's rest as they were exhausted, it was a long journey.

Before going to bed Jacques served them a simple dinner of bread, pea soup and salted lard accompanied by a glass of wine. "Thank you, Jacques, we were famished!" said Pierre.

They went to bed tired but contented, even Joseph was smiling at last.

The next morning was an early start again as they needed to set up all the goods where sales and trading were taking place.

As well as selling their goods Pierre was looking forward to buying a few items imported from France: dry beef, vinegar and wine. Catherine also insisted that he brought back flour, molasses and spices for cooking and baking.

Pierre was also determined to bring back some ornaments, *dentelle* and fine cloth for Catherine and Marguerite. He also wanted to get a pair of leather boots for himself which was quite an expensive luxury but well deserved, he thought. The trading and selling were going very well.

On the first day most of the furs were sold, fetching a really good price. The three of them were really excited and enjoying the banter going on between the buyers and sellers. In the evening they went back to the auberge tired but happy. After a nice meal they shared a few beers and gossip. Joseph felt really alive again being so busy helping. It made him forget for a while about his painful leg and the grief it brought him. What annoyed him most was the fact that after a busy day he was getting really bad aches and pains in his missing limb; how could it be that it was not there!

Baptiste, while sipping his beer, was confiding in them that he was soon going to ask Paulette's hand in marriage.

Pierre was delighted at the news. "You must tell your mother soon, she will be so pleased for you and I am sure Marguerite will be pleading for a new dress."

"From her own design I am sure and we'll never here the end of it," added Baptiste, laughing.

Joseph, encouraged by Baptiste's confidence, said: "I really like this girl in the village, her name is Dyani, she is beautiful."

"Did you speak to her?" Pierre asked.

"No way, why would she be interested in a cripple like me!" he answered with an angry tone.

"Don't you dare call yourself crippled, you are a fine-looking young man and very capable, look how much you helped us trading," Pierre told him firmly.

"Speak to her when we get back, you must or you will never know how she feels, be brave, Joseph," added Baptiste.

Joseph thought about what Baptiste just said. "I guess I have nothing to lose, I will speak to her."

On their last night in Montreal, after a very successful day of trades, most of the goods they had brought were sold including the vegetables and summer fruits. They decided to celebrate and try a few different taverns around the harbour. Joseph was really enjoying himself and was getting used to drinking alcohol which seems to make him more confident.

As they were entering a busy tavern for a last drink Joseph was a bit tipsy. Pierre said to him ,"Go and sit down, Baptiste and I will bring back the drinks. Beer again or do you want to try some *eau de vie*?"

"*Eau de vie*, please!" replied Joseph, smiling.

As Pierre and Baptiste were ordering the drinks at the crowded counter, a bunch of soldiers came to chat to Joseph. "What happened to you son, where you in the war?" one asked him.

"Yes," answered Joseph proudly

"I was fighting for my country."

"Good for you, brave man," answered the soldiers in chorus.

Two soldiers sat next to him wanting to know more and Joseph was more than happy to tell them. The soldiers told him they were here to build a new fort and protect the population against future attacks.

"A peace treaty has been signed but you never know, can you trust the English and the Iroquois? Our king does not think so," said one of the soldiers.

Another soldier sitting next to Joseph was older with silver hair and seemed to enjoy talking to Joseph.

As Pierre was walking back with the drinks to join them, he suddenly froze, he knew this older-looking soldier and could hardly believe it. Antoine himself! They looked at each other both with hatred in their eyes.

"Joseph, let's go, we're leaving," Pierre shouted, then he realised his mistake.

"Joseph? This is my son!" Antoine said to the other soldiers.

Pierre was livid. "Yes, your son from the family you abandoned!" he could not contain his anger.

"That's not true, son," he said, looking at Joseph. "I came back but Pierre met me in Montreal and told me your mother did not want me back."

"This a lie, you came back for business but never for your family and tell your son how when you went back you married someone else in France and had another family, you bigamous bastard!" Everyone in the tavern had stopped speaking, waiting for a big fight between the men.

To start with, Joseph was bewildered, not knowing who he should believe, what to say or what to do. The drinks had slowed his thoughts and reactions. He was stunned by the revelations. "Please, let's go, Joseph, come with us now," pleaded Pierre.

Without a word Joseph stood up, memories of his father departing, his mother crying and what really happened flooded in. It was Pierre he trusted, not this stranger of a father who left them. Whether it was the resentments he had kept for so long or the frustration of his maimed leg, he turned towards his father full of rage and started to hit him as hard as he could, swearing at him. "Scoundrel, scamp, devil. I hate you!"

Everyone stood there paralysed by the spectacle. Joseph kept hitting his father, striking blow after blow while his father was trying to protect himself but strangely not fighting back.

Did he feel deep inside he deserved it?

After what seems a long period of silence, many of the

soldiers intervened to stop Joseph. "Come on, man, that's enough, stop. He got the message, you better leave now."

Pierre and Baptiste grabbed Joseph to exit the tavern quickly to avoid more trouble.

They went back to Le Cheval Blanc but none of them could get to sleep. Pierre wanted to set sail as early as possible in the morning as he was so worried about this unfortunate encounter with Antoine. He was especially very concerned about Joseph and how it had affected him. Pierre also noticed how Antoine had collapsed after such a severe beating, hitting his head hard on the tavern counter on his fall, after all he was an older man now. As a soldier, if he was going to die of his injuries, Joseph could be arrested and in serious trouble. For killing a man, Joseph could be executed or at best sent to the galleys. Pierre felt it would be safer to be far away from this place. He wondered, however, why Antoine had decided to enrol in the French army and come back to Quebec.

On the trip back Joseph started to ask Pierre a lot of questions: "Is it true, did you meet my father before in Montreal?"

"Yes, I did," answered Pierre.

He explained the circumstances and what was said then. "Your father had not intention to come back to La Source and the men who knew him told me he had a new family in France. After the fight we had, I went to try to find him and talk to him but he ran away again," he added.

"I am sorry I never told you this before but you and Antoinette looked so settle, with Marie and Bidzill, I did not want you to know the truth that your father abandoned your mother and the two of you." He continued, "I preferred for you to believe your father perished at sea."

Joseph looked really sad after this revelation and answered, "I don't blame you, Pierre, don't worry. I just wish my father was dead."

Pierre was a fair-minded man and wanted to comfort Joseph. "When we were young your father and I were good friends, in fact we came to Quebec together tracking, hunting and fishing together for three years. We did really well and it was a very happy time for us, your father was strong, a very hard-working and able man. He was also great company; we had a lot of fun, I always felt safe with him in difficult situations because he was fearless when we encountered menacing indigenous tribes on their territories or greedy trackers who wanted to steel our finds. He was able to get us out of any difficult situations. I am not sure why he changed so much," added Pierre.

Joseph eyes lit up a bit hearing about his dad's youth. Pierre continued speaking about him. "When they met, your parents were truly in love with each other. After both your birth and Antoinette he was so proud and happy particularly with you, Joseph, he played and talked to you a lot as you were the eldest. He talked about you and him going fishing and hunting together in the future, he was a very good and supportive father to start with.

"Nobody understood why he left knowing the coming winter would be hard for your mother on her own. He became a restless man at the end and he gave such a lame excuse for his departure."

Pierre decided he had said everything he needed to say about Antoine and left it at that.

The homecoming

All the family was happy to see them back. Marguerite was waiting impatiently to see what presents her father had brought back for her and she marvelled when she saw the lovely lace and cloth for her new dress.

Pierre had also bought her a pair of leather shoes, it was the height of fashion for a young French woman. "Thank you, Papa, I love them."

Pierre smiled at her. She was a breath of fresh air, full of the joy of life. Catherine was pleased to see them back safe. She always worried when Pierre left for a few days. What happened to her late husband remained at the back of her mind. She embraced him tenderly, saying, "Glad to see you back."

Baptiste and Joseph unloaded the boat. "Don't forget to take back your presents for the village," shouted Baptiste to Joseph. "I'll accompany you back there after lunch."

Catherine, Pierre, the boys and Marguerite chatted over lunch. Marguerite wanted to know everything about their Montreal trip. They told her all about the bustle and hustle of trading and bartering, the stink of the fish near the harbour, the occasional popper trying to steal goods, and the lively taverns at night full of drunken men.

Pierre and the two boys, however, never mentioned meeting their encounter with Antoine. Pierre thought he would tell Catherine later in confidence. He was still worried about a warrant for Joseph if his father did not survive the attack so it was better to keep it quiet for now.

Marguerite was excited to hear all about Montreal.

"One day I'll go with you, Papa, it sounds wonderful. I can help you trade when I am older, I am good at counting you know." Everyone laughed, she was so enthusiastic about everything.

Early afternoon Joseph and Baptiste left for the indigenous village. Baptiste was very fond of Joseph and wanted to give him some support and encouragement after his ordeal. During the trip back they chatted about the fight at the inn.

"I understand what you did, I would have done the same as you if I had discovered my father had abandoned his family," Baptiste said to Joseph.

"He does not make me feel better you know and I thought it would. What if I killed him?"

"It is over, now in the past, try to think about the future, what about this girl Dyani? She sounds lovely, talk to her," insisted Baptiste, trying to cheer Joseph up.

Back at the village a gathering formed around Joseph to see what he had brought back from Montreal. The Hurons needed metal goods such as pans and knives and Joseph had traded many furs to bring back what they required. He also took back some of the luxury foods from France for Bidzill, Marie and Antoinette. He gave his sister a lovely hat he bought for her as a present. She was delighted with it and so grateful he had thought of it.

Joseph did not mention to anyone about meeting Antoine. Pierre had made a pact with Joseph and Baptiste asking them not to mention it to anyone for the time being. Pierre wanted to find out more about the aftermath of the fight. Did Antoine survive it? If he survived, was he going to ask the soldiers in Quebec to find his son and bring him to Justice?

Beating up a French soldier, especially a high-ranking soldier, was a very serious offence.

Antoine

Antoine was seriously injured and his two soldier friends took him to the hospital. He had lost consciousness after receiving several blows to the head and hitting the tavern's counter. The doctors did not know if he would make it. Antoine had always been a heavy drinker and his abuse of alcohol had taken its toll on his health over the years.

Back at the military fort the governor decided that the attack on one of his soldiers should be severely punished. "Find who is responsible at any cost," were his orders.

Only a few soldiers present at the inn, knew and heard what really happened. They felt guilty for not interfering earlier and stopping the fight but for them it was a family dispute between father and son, quite different from the usual drunken fights.

Meantime at the hospital, Antoine woke up. He was still

very poorly but conscious now. He could not move either his arms or legs; his head injuries had affected his mobility.

"I am finished," he murmured to the two soldiers who visited him.

The two soldiers were in charge of finding the culprit and wanted some information from Antoine.

"Tell us what happened? Who did that to you? We will find him and we promise you that he will be punished, probably hanged for such an attack on a high-ranking king's soldier."

Antoine's voice was very faint and the two men bent down to listen to what he had to say:

"It is not the lad's fault, I attacked him first and worst of all he is my son, injured and maimed fighting for his country, leave him alone. I don't want him prosecuted, he is the son I abandoned fifteen years ago! I deserve my fate."

The soldiers remained silent when Antoine added: "Please call the priest, I want to confess my sins before I die."

The priest came quickly and listened to Antoine's confession. Antoine received extreme unction before losing consciousness again.

An hour later Antoine took his last breath in hospital.

One will never know what Antoine thoughts were on his dying bed. Did he finally feel remorseful about abandoning his children and Marguerite? Was it his meeting with Joseph which triggered feelings for what he had been missing?

The soldiers took their findings back to the governor.

After listening to the report, the governor decided to follow Antoine's last wish not to prosecute his son.

Another reason the governor was now reluctant to pursue the matter, was the fact he knew Antoine had a wife and child in Nantes from an affluent and well-respected family. Prosecution would open all kind of unwanted information about Antoine's past; best left alone and buried, he concluded. The king would not take this information too kindly.

Antoine was buried in Montreal in a ceremony attended by all his garrison paying homage to his commanding authority and in defending the fort.

An official letter was sent to Victorine telling her Antoine was killed due to an unfortunate accident during the work carried out on Fort Marie. The letter said he was buried with full military honours. She was going to receive a rent from the king's purse to compensate for the loss of her husband.

Victorine and Helene were inconsolable; their beloved Antoine was dead. Victorine decided to move back to Paris with her parents for company. She was also hoping to help her cousin who was running the business. She thought that being on the shopfloor selling hats would help her get over her loneliness. Her father unfortunately passed away shortly after her move to Paris. She had to console her mother and look after Helene who was still missing Antoine. Her cousin had rejected her offer to help with the business. He was an old-fashioned man quite full of himself who thought women should stay at home.

He had no compassion for Victorine or anybody else, he was a very selfish man who never married.

Victorine resigned herself to look after her daughter's education and looking after her mother's failing health. She missed Antoine very much. In her eyes he was a loving husband and father who died to protect his king and country.

She would never know about Antoine's dark past that he had abandoned a wife and two children in Quebec.

He was a man who led a double life and mostly got away with it. Very respected in France by everyone and despised in Quebec for his behaviour by his best friends and son.

14

LIFE GOES ON

Pierre had noticed how Joseph could get into such a low mood since his accident, but even more so after his trip to Montreal.

Pierre told Catherine what had happened. She was horrified at first to hear that Antoine dared to come back and work in La Nouvelle-France, and when she heard about the fight between father and son, she screamed with tears in her eyes:

"Poor Joseph, it must have been so upsetting and shocking to meet his father after thinking he was probably dead," she continued. "Hearing the truth about him and how he deserted his family, no wonder Joseph decided to hit him; the memory of his distraught mother explains his anger!"

Pierre and Catherine decided it would be wise to inform Marie and Bidzill about the event, and a meeting was set up between them to discuss the situation. Marie, like Catherine, felt enraged when she heard the story. Both women were thinking about Marguerite, abandoned by Antoine, who died of a broken heart.

Pierre calmly explained that Antoine seemed severely injured after the fight. If he died, there would be severe consequences for Joseph. Antoine was a high-ranking soldier.

They could already be looking for Joseph in the French king's army.

The four of them came to the decision that it would be a good idea for Pierre and Bidzill to travel back to Montreal for a few days and see what they could discretely find out; perhaps they could casually chat to some of the soldiers in the taverns without drawing too much attention.

Marie and Catherine, meantime, tried to find ways of cheering Joseph up without mentioning what they knew about his trip to Montreal.

Baptiste had told his mother that Joseph was secretly in love with Dyani. Still, he had been too afraid to talk to her. Marie came up with the idea of organising a fete in the Indian village for young people coming of age. She thought of a few games where young men and women would have to take part and interact, and she would also teach them some of the new dances popular in France.

The fete was a great success. Catherine also took part and brought Marguerite and her two younger teenage boys.

Joseph, at the beginning of the party, looked morose and reluctant to take part. When Marie paired him with Dyani during the dancing learning sessions, she finally saw him smile and enjoy himself; he seemed transformed.

Joseph and Dyani were shy at the start, but after a while and a few laughs doing a wrong step, they relaxed and talked. "Do you like dancing?" Joseph asked Dyani using the Huron dialect as she did not speak French.

"I am not good, but it is fun." She smiles.

"I am the one who stepped on your toes with my lame leg," Joseph said, smiling.

"Let's sit down," she says. "I'll show you what I really like to do. Give me a minute." She returned to her family quarters with a bundle of beautiful beaded bracelets and necklaces.

"Look, I love making those, choosing the colours and the beads. I also make belts; I will make one, especially for you," she adds.

Joseph was impressed; she showed such passion for her craft. "I know you are a courageous man. You fought with my tribe, the Hurons; we are all so proud of you," she told Joseph. "I am so honoured to finally meet you."

He felt much more confident hearing it from her. From that day onwards, Joseph and Dyani spent a lot of time together under the watchful eyes of Dyani's mother.

From then on, Joseph loved sitting peacefully near the hominy hole to spend time with Dyani while she was grinding corn or making jewellery.

Joseph looked much happier and started to be his old self, participating in many activities to help Bidzill and his men. The change in him was for everyone to see. He talked and laughed a lot more; his confidence was back. Marie, Pierre and his family were relieved to see him happy again and more optimistic about his future; he was in love, and Dyani reciprocated his feelings. One day, she confided in him, "I wanted to be close to you since the first time I saw you in the village." Joseph was so happy to hear it.

He never mentioned his encounter with his father to anyone and especially did not tell Antoinette. He wanted to protect his sister from the truth as it had shocked him to realise his father's deceitful behaviour. He had really abandoned them. Antoinette believed her father had probably died at sea. Joseph thought it was better not to reveal to his sister the sad truth: their father had abandoned them, never looking back.

Occasionally, he wondered if his father was still alive after their fight, and he felt a bit guilty that his father did not fight back. Why, he asked himself?

Marie had started a school in the Indian village and enjoyed spending more time with her children. Antoinette was helping her by teaching religion. Antoinette's moody behaviour had shifted, and Marie wondered if it was because she saw her brother being happier. Toinette also was closer to Marie now as they worked together. They shared funny anecdotes about the children. They could laugh together and share their thoughts.

Huron children found some of the French words challenging to pronounce, particularly words containing the letter r, such as "*truite*", "*crème*" or "Marie". With the children's mispronunciation, the words became "*tuite*", "*ceme*" and "Ma-e".

Sometimes, the children and some adult Indian-

Huron would miss out on articles before nouns. Instead of saying "*le bateau*," they simply used "*bateau*".

Antoinette and Marie thought it was very amusing. Still, they never ridiculed the children and adults or embarrassed them.

Marie was delighted with her growing new bond with Antoinette. It was like having back a part of her beloved sister. The school was a great success as most of the Huron children and Marie's children were bilingual, speaking French as well as the Huron dialect.

Huron dialect called Wyandot was more accessible and easier to learn than French. However, Marie's children sometimes struggled with Wyandot words with the letter "w", such as "*weeish*", meaning five. French grammar and pronunciation, however, were trickier to learn.

The Catholic church, run by the Jesuits, was delighted with such progress and to see so many indigenous children converted to Christianity. It was a pleasure for everyone to see the children sitting cross legged on the grass in the summer, listening to Marie or Antoinette and repeating words in a flayed chorus. Every time the priests or the nuns visited the Huron village, they were delighted to see so many Huron children becoming good Christians.

While Marie and Catherine organised the fete in the Indian village to get Joseph out of his melancholy, Pierre and Bidzill left for Montreal. They did not want to raise Joseph's suspicion, so Bidzill announced that the fishing season had been so good that he needed to sell the big surplus to the Montreal market with Pierre's help.

Once in Montreal, they stayed in Pierre's usual inn, Le Cheval Blanc. The first night, they went around drinking beer in the taverns around the harbour and trying to get some information about the sergeant major who was beaten up a few weeks earlier, without attracting too much attention. Bidzill was not used to drinking and was very nervous going from tavern to tavern, worried about drinking too much and being provoked into a fight as a native. Some drunk and aggressive men were snarling at him, calling him "*Peau-Rouge*".

Pierre, luckily, was with him to calm the situation. "Look, we don't want any trouble; we're just looking for a friend," he would tell them.

Pierre did not recognise any of the soldiers he had seen previously, and they went back to their inn empty-handed.

The next evening, Jacques, the tavern owner, suggested they should try a tavern called Le Roi Louis, situated in one of the narrow lanes leading away from the harbour. "A lot of the soldiers are drinking there at the moment. It seems to be their latest meeting place."

Pierre and Bidzill headed to the tavern, hopeful. Nothing happened for the first hour; Pierre and Bidzill sat chatting and drinking in a corner. *There are a lot of soldiers here, but nobody with a familiar face*, thought Pierre. He headed to the bar to order a couple of beers when one of the soldiers shouted at him, "Hey, are you not the fellow who was with the cripple who beat the hell out of his father four weeks ago?"

Pierre froze, not knowing what to say.

The soldier continued, "You know the old guy died

from his injuries. Would you believe there will be no court case! He confessed to a priest it was all his fault for abandoning his family in Quebec."

The soldier looked at Pierre's stricken face and added, "Don't worry, man, the guy was a bigamist. It would have been too embarrassing for the army to pursue the case."

Pierre sat down again, speechless. Without asking anyone, they found out so much information. They left the tavern quickly and returned to Le Cheval Blanc, still stunned by the news. It felt like an enormous weight off their shoulders hearing the news.

The two men were relieved to hear that the authorities would not be looking for Joseph, and Joseph was now free from prosecution. On the other hand, they had not wished for Antoine to die and were worried about telling the others back in Quebec.

They were unsure how to inform Joseph that his father had died, as they knew he had already felt guilty.

Joseph had told them after the fight, "I hit him too hard, and he never fought back. He is an old man, but I was so angry with him! I don't know what came over me; it was like I was possessed and I could not stop."

They decided they would tell the truth about Antoine's death.

When Pierre and Bidzill arrived, they first spoke to their wives to explain what had happened and why they returned to Montreal. Afterwards, they both talked to Joseph. To soften the news, they pointed out that his father was not killed during the fight but died later in hospital from an infected wound. They added, "Your father also confessed his sins to a priest during his stay in hospital. He was sorry about abandoning you in Quebec and said the reason for the fight was all his fault. He died in peace after his confession."

Pierre and Bidzill had decided to never mention the one thing that could really upset Joseph and Antoinette: the news that Antoine had married again in France and had a daughter. They thought it would be too painful for Antoinette and Joseph. It was better to let it rest.

Joseph did not know what to say and sighed.

He was not sure how he felt at this very moment. It was a mixture of overwhelming guilt and, at the same time, feelings of having avenged his mother's death. It was all very confusing for him.

Time passed, and life and trading in the Indian village were flourishing. Joseph had come to terms with the death of his father and one day had told his sister, Antoinette, now old enough at almost fifteen to understand. Antoinette kindly said, "I am proud of you, Joseph, and I am glad at the end that our father confessed and regretted leaving us."

They would never know about Antoine having another family in France. It was for the best.

Joseph and Dyani were preparing their wedding for the summer. The preparations had taken over two years because the Catholic church had instructed that Dyani should be baptised and then prepared to receive communion before any wedding could take place. It took so long because Dyani had to be taught French first, as Marie's school started when Dyani was already fourteen.

The marriage finally took place in June. Joseph and Dyani were now eighteen years old. The weather was glorious that day, and the couple were beaming, filled with joy and happiness when they left the church. There was a lot of dancing and singing in the Indian village, everybody celebrated the young couple.

Bidzill and Marie were very proud of Joseph. They considered him their son, and Joseph was doing so well now after overcoming so much pain in his young life.

What really touched Bidzill and Marie was when Joseph approached them after the ceremony and said, "Thank you so much for your support and everything you have done for me. I could not wish for a better family; you have always been there for me and Antoinette, I love you both very much."

After hearing this, Marie was in tears, tears of joy. Both Marie and Bidzill were so touched by Joseph's kind words.

Catherine and Pierre attended the wedding. The event was joyful; they were happy to witness so much love and happiness. It was not long ago that they celebrated Baptiste and Paulette's wedding in May.

Philippe, who had become the local priest, had officiated the ceremony. Pierre and Catherine hoped to be grandparents soon after the couple was married.

In the last few months, however, they had grown worried about their younger son Robert, who was now twenty. His behaviour was erratic, and they found him very drunk a few times, lying in the outside barn. He was becoming very rude to his parents and people around him, even to his young sister Marguerite, whom he used to dote on. She often talked about him to her parents with tears in her eyes, distraught to be so nastily dismissed: "He told me to buzz off again and to shut up. Why is he so nasty to me?"

Marguerite could not understand the change in her big brother as they were so close before. She was terribly upset, not knowing how to bring back the close bond they used to have. Baptiste gave up talking to his younger brother after Robert told him to mind his own business. Baptiste asks him several times to help him run the farm, but Robert dismisses him every time, belittling him: "I'll do better than being a farmer; I can read and write, you can't." Baptiste thought he had better things to do now he was married and was put off by his brother's nastiness.

Paul, his youngest brother, had given up totally on Robert. He was a quiet, dreamy, easy-going boy who liked to work outdoors on the farm or fish and hunt. He kept his distance from Robert, and perhaps it was a way of protecting himself from his brother's evil influence and behaviour.

Robert also had been fighting with other young men in taverns around Quebec. He gained quite a reputation as a bad-tempered drunk. He was a tall and robust young man looking older than his twenty years.

Catherine tried to ask him, "What's happening to you, Robert? You have changed so much in the last few months. Please talk to me."

"Leave me alone. I am a man now; I can do what I want," he replied.

"Why do you drink so much? What's wrong?" she continues with a sad voice. "You need to pull your weight around here and help us more to run the farm."

"I don't care about that stupid farm." Following this nasty remark, Robert stormed out.

It had become a pattern: Robert would leave for two or three weeks at a time and come back to sleep in the outside barn for two or three days without saying a word to anyone there.

Catherine was so worried about him that she brought him food and clean clothes in the barn without reprimanding him, frightened that he would never return if she did.

He had lost a lot of weight, and big shadows were under his eyes. The whole family was so worried about him that they were at a loss about what to do. Philippe had come over from the parsonage a few times to talk to his brother but to no avail. He gave up as his brother, each time, would bow his head down and remain mute. The last time he left him, Philippe said, "I'll pray for you," and left.

Three months passed, and Robert had not returned once to "Les Trois Rivieres". Catherine and the family were getting increasingly concerned.

When a soldier sent by the fort master came to the farm to see Pierre and Catherine, they knew it was bad news.

The soldiers had found Robert dead in an alleyway near the port of Quebec. He had been beaten to death;

however, the authorities had not discovered the culprit. They suspected the reason was a gambling debt Robert had been unable to repay.

Catherine was devasted losing another son again. After Nicolas's death, she never thought she would lose another son. It was more than Catherine could bear. She was distraught, and Pierre had to carry her back inside the house as she collapsed after the dreadful news.

The whole family was in shock, feeling guilty, all wondering what they could have done to prevent his demise.

Philippe was overwhelmed with grief and said, "I am a priest. Despite his silence and stubbornness, I should have helped him." He started crying quietly.

Marguerite remained silent but felt so helpless and sad.

Baptiste also felt tremendous guilt; he could have been more present and understanding with his brother as they used to be so close. He had been fed up with Robert's smug comments about him, but he should have known better. His brother was in trouble and was hiding it as a proud man.

Pierre also had tried to talk to Robert on many occasions, trying to talk him into sense; however, each time, he was told, "You are not my father; it is none of your business."

The funeral took place the week after. Robert's body was placed next to his brother Nicolas. Apart from the church hymns and the priest's kind words, you could hear the sobs of family and friends. Philippe had not wished to officiate the service, preferring to support his mother and sister.

Pierre and Baptiste sat behind them, lost in their own thoughts and guilt. They reflected on Robert's sad end and wondered if they could have done more to prevent it.

Bidzill, Marie and the children all came to the service intensely sad, knowing how hard it is to lose a loved one.

It took a few months for Catherine to smile again; she had been very morose. She spent days lying in bed, not looking after herself. Pierre and Marguerite took turns attending to her, bringing her food and drinks. Marguerite would brush her mother's hair every morning and night and clean her face, chatting away, trying to cheer her up.

Philippe and Baptiste also took turns to see her and talk to her.

Philippe mentioned to her that he had seen many men and a few women with drinking problems in his parish, and it was arduous to help convince them to stop drinking and gambling. "Ultimately, it has to be their own decision, Mum, you cannot do it for them." He also told his mother how guilty he felt about not helping Robert more. "We all feel guilty, Mum. It is because we loved him and cared for him, but I am not sure we could have done more. I am at peace with it now and hope you will too," he concluded.

They had never seen Catherine so downbeat and gloomy before, except after Nicolas's death; she usually was such a strong and cheerful person.

With time and support from each other, the family came to terms with Robert's death.

Catherine carried on helping Pierre and Baptiste with the farm and business. She knew she would never really be over the death of her two sons, but she had to carry on for the rest of the family. Marguerite and Pierre were always so supportive. Marie and Bidzill also visited her as often as they could; Catherine felt very fortunate to have them. She now kept a watchful eye on Marguerite, who had become a stunning young teenager with many young men courting her. Both Pierre and her did not want her to fall for a man who could not look after her well. Marguerite now belonged to an affluent family, and her parents were wary of some young men trying to get her attention. Some were very handsome and charming, but what were their intentions?

Would they genuinely love and cherish their daughter? While most families in Quebec wanted to marry their daughter off at any cost, it was not the wish of Pierre and Catherine.

15

Epilogue

Marie was now embracing the Huron way of life completely. She felt so settled in the village that she seldom returned to the convent. Now she was older, she felt fulfilled with teaching in the community and looking after her children. The twins Anne and Louis were growing up fast, and Louis often accompanied his father during the hunting and fishing season.

Anne helped the other Huron girls make bead necklaces and bracelets.

Occasionally, she also enjoyed fishing with her father and brother. It was an unusual activity for a girl then.

Anne also learned to make pots and bowls and decorate them with plant-based paint. She loved collecting and using shells; it was another one of her hobbies. It was her favourite task. However, she could have been more enthusiastic about helping with cooking duties, though she still had to help grind corn, gather food, and prepare vegetables.

Marie's younger children were still at the playing stage, totally immersed in Huron culture.

Marie had started dressing as a Huron woman regularly. She wore decorative clothing adorned with colourful beads and fur strips around her back and neck in the winter months. She also greased her silvery hair as she found it an easy hairstyle to keep.

What Marie loved about the Huron-Wyandot culture was that women had an essential role in their community. It was a matrilineal kinship system. Children were considered born to the mother's family and took their status from her.

It was usually so different from the French system, where the men had all the rights, and the women had none regarding status. As a mature and knowledgeable woman in the community, she could influence the elders and leaders of the Huron village.

She was respected and consulted to give advice.

Marie was also the medicine lady in the village. She knew so much about illnesses and wounds that everybody trusted her judgment. She played a prominent role in the community, and Bidzill was still very proud of her. She was also consulted by other friendly indigenous tribes for her wisdom regarding health and other matters.

She did not shy away either from other duties usually carried out by women.

She cooked, sewed, and cleaned out the fire hearth. Marie also enjoyed making baskets, weaving mats and fishing nets. Those were some new tasks she had to learn living with the Hurons.

Every now and then, she reflected on her life, thinking how lucky she was and how her life in La Nouvelle-France exceeded her expectations.

Twice a year, she would go to her sister's grave. Once in the spring in May with Antoinette and Joseph to mark Marguerite's birthday. They brought flowers, and the children asked Marie to reminisce about their mother.

In September, before the cold winter set in, Marie would go alone and talk to her sister. It was a special time to keep her sister's memory alive, and she cherished these moments.

Marie would tell Marguerite how much she missed her and how grateful she was that she had brought her to Quebec.

"I have a wonderful, loving husband, my children are my pride and joy, healthy and bright and, most of all, I have a career, and I do a job I could never have dreamed of when I came here. Thank you, my dear sister," Marie said.

Marie also told her how well her children were doing: "Joseph is married now and very happy with his wife Dyani; I think it won't be long before they start a family.

"Antoinette is a brilliant young woman; she teaches the Huron children with me; she is a clever and lively girl who knows her mind. You would be so proud of them both."

She would tell her sister everything and found speaking to her very calming and appeasing.

She would mention how well Pierre and Catherine were doing with their farm and building business. The sadness for them of losing another son but how delighted they were with young Marguerite, a fun and determined young lady.

Marie was very proud to be her godmother and felt she saw a bit of herself in young Marguerite. Catherine's sons, Baptiste and Paul, were also flourishing. Baptiste was married and very successful with Pierre's construction business. Paul was an outdoorsy young man who loved fishing and hunting.

Marie missed her sister but had come to terms with her death. With age and experience, she realised that a few women could become very depressed and even lose their minds after giving birth. Many women improved, but a few never recovered and were left alone, often considered mad.

Marie knew there was no cure at the moment but was hoping one day, women would be helped by medicine.

Some Huron medicine women later used a plant with yellow flowers to make a drink they gave to women who experienced low moods after giving birth. Many women seemed to recover after a few weeks. She wished Marguerite had tried it; she might still be here with her.

The two sisters had sailed for "La Nouvelle-France" over twenty-five years ago, looking for a new and better life.

Marguerite had fulfilled her wish to marry, but unfortunately, married life did not turn out well for her. Nevertheless, she had given birth to two fantastic children who were prospering in this new land.

For Marie, who had been so nervous about following her sister to Quebec, life had been beyond her expectations.

She had never imagined that one day she would meet and fall in love with a Huron called Bidzill, marry him, have children and live a happy life among the Huron tribe.

Marie smiled thinking about her life journey and how lucky her children were to be in such a sheltered environment, being loved by their parents and the community, being well fed and healthy with a promising future despite the cold winter weather. Once her children are older, one day, she will tell them about her journey with her sister from a French orphanage to a new land called Quebec. She wondered what the future holds for them once she is gone but was very optimistic it can only get brighter.

She told herself, "I have no regret leaving my motherland. Quebec is my home, and I genuinely love my life here." Still, she shed a tear thinking about Marguerite.